P9-DMG-583

TAKEN BY PASSION

TAKEN BY PASSION

JAYMIE HOLLAND

St. Martin's Griffin
New York

This is a work of fiction. All of the characters, organizations, and events portrayed in this novel are either products of the author's imagination or are used fictitiously.

www.stmartins.com

Book design by Anna Gorovoy

ISBN 978-0-312-38666-5

First published in e-book format in the United States under the title Wonderland: *King of Hearts* by Ellora's Cave Publishing, Inc.

First St. Martin's Griffin Edition: August 2011

10 9 8 7 6 5 4 3 2 1

AUTHOR'S NOTE

Dear Reader,

The Wonderland series is back! *Taken by Passion* is the first book in the four-book erotica series originally published with an e-publisher as Wonderland: *King of Hearts* by Cheyenne McCray. It is published in its entirety.

This award-winning, bestselling romantic erotica Wonderland series is being re-published under the name Jaymie Holland to clearly distinguish it from other works by me. I believe it is important my readers know that when they read this series it is extreme erotica in nature compared to other books by me they may have read before.

Taken by Passion, as Wonderland: *King of Hearts,* won numerous awards and accolades, including the RT Book Reviews Reader's Choice Award for Best Erotic Romance and Erotica of 2003.

Some of *King of Hearts'* other awards include The

Road to Romance's Reviewer's Choice Award, the Gold Star Award from *Just Erotic Romance Reviews,* and the Cupid and Psyche Award from *The Romance Studio.*

King of Hearts received many accolades, among them, five roses from *A Romance Review,* five hearts from *The Romance Studio,* and it was a four-and-a-half-star Top Pick from *RT Book Reviews.* Many review sites gave it high praise, including *The Best Reviews, Round Table Reviews,* and *Romance Reviews Today.*

I hope you enjoy *Taken by Passion* and have fun on your trip down the rabbit hole.

Cheyenne McCray
aka Jaymie Holland

TAKEN BY PASSION

PROLOGUE

It had been the morning from hell. Possibly the worst day of her life, but Alice O'Brien was still reserving judgment on that one.

A thick San Francisco fog shrouded the city, perfectly mirroring her dark mood as she stood on the landing outside her apartment door and searched her purse. She'd just climbed the three flights to her apartment, which was above the dim sum restaurant on Grant Street, and had managed to snag her last pair of queen-sized nylons because *somebody* had left a mop bucket out on the second floor landing.

Damn but she had to get a new apartment and a new landlady.

And of course, before that lovely icing on her day, when she'd made the hike from her *ex*-job on Market Street, all the way up to Grant, she'd stumbled into possibly the deepest puddle in the whole freaking city. And definitely the most polluted.

Alice shivered, her toes growing numb in her soaked walking shoes. *Now where's that damn key?* After this morning, it would be just peachy if she'd gone and lost her house key.

Normally Alice would be at work right now, efficiently performing mundane secretarial duties for Mitch, that slimeball of an accountant she used to work for. However, when she'd insisted this morning that her name was not Monica and that he was not the president and that her secretarial duties did not include sucking his cock he'd canned her.

The bastard had freaking fired her!

Well, he'd be one cock-less sonofabitch CPA when her twin sister, Alexi, got ahold of him. A dynamic attorney, Alexi specialized in sexual harassment, and Alice fully intended to hire her and make that bastard pay.

Alice gave a cry of frustration and almost threw her purse onto the cracked concrete landing. Where was that damn key?

A splatter landed on Alice's shoulder. Very slowly she turned to look, knowing what would be on her trench coat even before she saw it.

Pigeon shit.

Alice groaned and banged her forehead against the wooden door of her apartment.

Perfect. Just perfect.

How could the day possibly get any worse?

She banged her head against the door, harder this time. It swung open and she stumbled over the thresh-

2

old, barely managing to keep from falling on her face. Smells of stale bacon and moldy carpet assailed her.

Damn Jon. Her somewhat forgetful—make that irresponsible—fiancé had forgotten to lock the door again.

Well, this time it might be the one thing in the whole miserable morning that had worked out in her favor.

Alice ached from head to toe as she dropped her purse on the telephone stand just inside the entryway, then pulled the door shut behind her. Who would have thought that being fired, falling into a puddle the size of the San Francisco Bay, and shredding her best and most expensive pair of pantyhose—not to mention getting shit on—would be so exhausting?

And all before noon.

After she shrugged out of her soiled trench coat, she let it drop to the cracked black-and-white-checked linoleum. She kicked off her soaked walking shoes and peeled off her sopping wet nylons. Her low-heeled sandals were in her purse—everyone in the City by the Bay made the hike up and down the steep hills in comfortable shoes and carried their heels for work. With its narrow streets and lack of inexpensive parking, no one drove to work in San Francisco. Instead they walked or took the city buses or rode the cable cars.

Alice gave a weary sigh as she tugged on her short skirt that had somehow twisted around her ample hips so that the zipper was off kilter. Why couldn't she be slender, with all those thick, wavy, auburn locks like her twin? Alice wouldn't have minded at all if they'd been identical, so long as they both looked like Alexi. The only thing they had in common was their turquoise eyes.

Alice sighed again as she tightened the blue silk ribbon holding her hair back, away from her rounder-than-Alexi's face. She lifted her fine, long, and very straight blond hair out of the collar of her blouse and eyed the old-fashioned telephone.

She took a deep breath, snatched up the receiver, and dialed Alexi's cell phone. *Just wait until she hears what happened!*

"This is Alexi," came the firm don't-mess-with-me voice that she used for business.

"It's your favorite twin," Alice said as she fiddled with the woven bracelet her sister had given her for their eighteenth birthday, six years ago.

Alexi's tone changed instantly to that of the friendly, fun-loving sister Alice had grown up with: "Heya, sis. Dump that loser yet?"

Alice rolled her eyes to the ceiling of the small entryway. Neither her best friend, Maryam, nor her sister liked Jon at all. They didn't see the fun side of him and the way he made Alice laugh. "You're talking about my fiancé."

Alexi snorted. "Yeah. The loser."

"Whatever." Alice twirled the phone cord like a mini jump rope. "I'm calling from home. Are you down at the office or working out of your apartment today?"

"Right upstairs." Papers rustled as Alexi spoke. "Shall I stomp twice?"

"You don't happen to have any mocha almond fudge in your freezer, do you?" Alice pulled the phone cord taut in irritation. "Jon ate the last of mine. And damn it, I need to talk."

"Two whole pints. Is this a pint-each talk, or a two-spoons-in-one-pint problem?"

"Honey, I need a pint all my own." Alice tapped her long fingernails on the telephone stand, the *click-clack* echoing through the empty hallway. "Something happened today—"

"What?" Alice could just imagine Alexi bolting out of her chair as she practically shouted the word. "You're not hurt or anything, are you? I would have sensed it—"

"No." She had to smile at her two-minute-older protective sister. "It's nothing like that. It—"

A woman's passionate cry tore through the apartment and Alice froze.

"What was that?" Alexi asked in her attorney voice.

"Hold on." Alice's heart pounded and she gritted her teeth. "I'm about to find out."

She thunked the phone on the wooden stand, and as she walked away she could hear her sister's voice saying, "Alice? You'd better be back on the line in thirty seconds or I'm coming down with the Mace!"

Alice's head buzzed as her bare feet padded over the cracked linoleum floor toward the single bedroom. *He couldn't. He wouldn't.*

Would he?

Feminine laughter followed by Jon's familiar moan of ecstasy confirmed that he would. *The cheating bastard.*

But she had to see for herself. Had to see that it was her loser of a fiancé . . .

She peeked around the door frame, and the buzzing in her head increased. Sure enough, Jon was naked and between the just-as-naked thighs of Min, their beautiful slender landlady, and he was suckling the dark nipples of her small, firm breasts.

And worse yet, they were on Alice's bed. The bed she'd had since she was a teenager and taken with her when she'd moved away from home.

That was her bed!

Alice wanted to scream, but she was too stunned to move. It was happening again. Goddamn it, again. Catching her last boyfriend screwing around apparently hadn't been enough.

"You ready to be fucked?" Min asked Jon, her sultry dark eyes filled with lust.

"Oh yeah, babe." Jon flipped his dark red hair out of his eyes as he grabbed his dick in his hand and positioned it at Min's slit. "I wanna be fucked good."

"This is some fine shit," a man's deep baritone came from near the chest of drawers behind the bedroom door, and the buzzing in Alice's head reached epic proportions.

Her jaw dropped as a big man with a full beard walked into the center of the room. The guy was partially clothed in leather chaps, thick-linked silver chains, and a spiked collar. He had greased his dick with something and was stroking his hand up and down his erection with one palm while carrying a leather strap and chain in his other hand.

Alice caught the scent of roses and she sucked in her

breath. The asshole was using *her* expensive rose-scented body cream.

Before she'd recovered from that revelation, O-bearded-one reached Min and Jon, who were still fondling each other on Alice's bed.

She couldn't believe it. Jon was engaging in a ménage à trois—fulfilling Alice's fantasy for another woman.

When Alice had told Jon that her most erotic fantasy was to be tied up and taken by two men at once, he'd laughed and told her that would never happen. He'd said she'd have to settle for his dick in her pussy and her favorite glass cock up her ass, because he wasn't going there. So she'd experimented with various toys and butt plugs and used her imagination for the rest.

And here the bastard was, about to help Min have it from both ends.

Only the big bearded guy came up behind Jon's skinny ass and gave it a few quick slaps with his palm. "You ready, Jon-boy?"

Jon-boy?

"Do it to me, Stone."

Do it to me, Stone?

Alice stared in horrified fascination as Stone bent over Jon, yanked his head back and fastened the leather strap around her *ex*-fiancé's neck, and let the attached long, thick-linked silver chain lie across Jon's back. Stone unhooked one of the chains hanging from his black chaps—the chain had two clamps on it. Just as she wondered what in the heck he was going to do with that, Stone handed it to Min. The woman proceeded to clamp each of Jon's nipples, and when she tugged on the chain Jon cried out like a stuck pig.

"Does that hurt, slave?" Min asked.

"Yeah." Jon's voice squeaked. "Hurts real good, babe."

Min frowned and curled her lip into a snarl. "From this point forward you will call me Mistress and you shall refer to Stone as Master. Do you understand, slave?"

"Yes, Mistress." Jon's breathing grew more labored, and he had an excited glaze to his eyes and flush to his cheeks. "Yes, Master."

Oh. My. God.

Alice's soon to be ex- and *dead* fiancé was a freaking submissive. When it came to sex, she didn't mind a few beta characteristics in a man, although she preferred alpha—a combination was nice.

"I will allow you to fuck me, slave." Min's exotic eyes narrowed. She pulled taut on the chains and Jon blanched. "But you will not come until I tell you to. Is that clear, slave?"

"Yes, Min." When she yanked on the chains Jon cried out and hurriedly said, "I mean, yes, Mistress."

While he reached around Jon's hips, Stone pressed his erection to the slave's ass. He grabbed Jon's dick, none too gently, and snapped on a leather cuff close to his balls.

"Feels good, don't it, slave?" Stone's bass voice rumbled.

Jon squeaked again. "Real good."

Stone grabbed the long chain hanging from the collar and smacked Jon's ass with it, hard enough to leave a red welt, and Jon yelped.

"Master!" Jon shouted. "I mean, real good, Master!"

Stone took his well-lotioned erection and placed it to Jon's tight red anus. "This is going to hurt, and you're going to love it, aren't you, slave?"

Licking his lips, Jon replied, "Yes, Master."

"Slide your dick into Min's pussy." Stone slapped the chain across Jon's ass.

Jon responded with another yelp and a, "Yes, Master!" and then plunged his dick into Min.

"Very good, slave," she said as she tugged on the nipple clamps. "Now, when Stone takes you, I want you to fuck me without stopping. If you stop then I shall be forced to punish you. Do you understand?"

"Yes, Mistress."

Alice couldn't believe how excited Jon looked. He was obviously enjoying every bit of this Dom/sub routine and was totally getting off on it. Part of her wondered if she should just turn and walk away, but part of her wanted to see just how far Jon would let this go.

In the next second she found out as Stone yanked the chain to Jon's collar and pulled it tight as he plunged his dick into Jon's ass and began pummeling him unmercifully.

Jon literally screamed.

"How do you like that, slave?" Stone shouted as he fucked Jon's ass and whipped him at the same time with the chain.

"I love it, Master," Jon said, tears rolling down his face.

Min yanked on the nipple clamps and Jon cried out again. "Sorry, Mistress," he said, and began fucking her with his sorry-excuse-for-a-prick. "That hurts so good, Master and Mistress."

"Oh. My. God." Alexi's hoarse whisper startled Alice from her horrified trance.

Her gaze shot to her twin's and she saw Alexi holding her can of Mace like she was about to spray a giant cockroach. A really grotesque man-eating roach. Alice knew by the look on Alexi's face that Jon was going to be hurting a hell of a lot more once she got through with him.

"You cheating sonofabitch." Alexi's courtroom attorney's voice cut through the kink happening on Alice's bed.

All kink instantly ceased. The three froze as their gazes riveted on Alice and Alexi.

"Shit," Jon muttered.

Alice eyed him more coolly than she ever thought possible. "You mean shit, *Mistress*."

And with that she spun and marched away. She had to get out of the house, now. Hell, she'd never be able to sleep in that bed again, much less this apartment.

Behind her she heard Alexi laying into the slimy bastard. Alice had no doubt that the apartment would be cleared of all scum in no time flat.

The buzzing in her head was coming real close to migraine level. Alice slipped on a pair of dry walking shoes, yanked on her San Francisco Giants baseball jacket, and grabbed her purse off the stand where the telephone receiver still hung from its cord.

In the background, she heard Jon's defensive whine as he started, "If Alice wasn't so fat, I wouldn't have to—"

A spraying sound and Alexi's shout of, "Bastard!" covered up the rest of the dick's words as she let loose with the Mace. Shrieks and screams from club kink immediately followed.

Without looking back, without closing the door behind her, Alice fled into the dreary San Francisco morning.

CHAPTER ONE

KING JARRONN SCRUBBED HIS HAND OVER HIS light beard and flexed his powerful muscles as he scowled at the four cards lying facedown on the *a'bin*. The cards mocked him from the glowing table Sorceress Kalina used to foretell the destiny of all four kingdoms throughout the lands of Tarok.

Beside him the sorceress shifted and a red crystal heart dangled from each of her erect nipples, both hearts glittering in the candlelight. "It is time to choose, Milord."

Jarronn growled and glared at the cards. *How can I simply turn a card when the fate of my kingdom rests at my fingertips?* The king clenched his fists and bit back a snarl. *It is too simple a gesture for the destiny of my people.*

He shifted his attention from the *a'bin* to the cobalt walls of the sorceress's private chamber. Where the rest of his kingdom was bright and airy, Kalina's quarters were dark and mysterious, mirroring the sorceress herself. A thousand scents flooded the king's acute senses . . . honeysuckle incense, tallow, perfumes, oils, elixirs, and more perplexing smells that surely only the sorceress could identify.

Candle flame danced and flickered in the gentle breeze that moved through the lone window and across Jarronn's naked chest. Sheer pearl veiling fluttered to either side of the large window that offered a stunning view of his realm. In contrast to his dark thoughts, outside sunlight warmed brilliant flowers in the royal rainbow gardens and teased forth new growth. Birds, squirrels, chipmunks, and every other animal species mated with spring fervor, sowing countless seeds for a new crop of babes. Many of Jarronn's subjects frolicked throughout the extensive gardens, naked as they were wont to be, enjoying one another's pleasures.

It should have been a time of growth for Jarronn's people, too—a time for males to seed their mates' wombs. A time to look forward to new births in the fall.

Veins rose along the surface of Jarronn's muscles as rage filled him anew that he had been unable to break Mikaela's powerful mindspells . . . the black sorcery that had rendered the women of Tarok incapable of conception for nearly two decades.

His failure to end this mind-war wrenched at Jarronn's soul. He clenched his fist and raised it toward the south, where the bitch's realm crouched like a great swamp beast beneath the Malachad Mountains. Damn the skies, but he would find some way to end Mikaela's reign of black sorcery.

What Kalina offered the kings of Tarok . . . how could such magic possibly be their salvation?

Mayhap the spring will be a time of renewal once again. The thought stirred within him, and he growled.

"You must choose one, Milord," Kalina said, a hint of urgency in her melodic voice.

Jarronn turned his scowl on the lovely sorceress, but her eyes were lowered in the proper position of respect, her stance wide and her hands clasped behind her back. A fine red glitter powdered the surface of her kohl-lined eyelids. The red crystal hearts sparkled as they swung from each of her berry-dark nipples, and a crimson leather collar enhanced Kalina's slender neck. Long black hair tumbled over her pale breasts.

A primal urge roared through Jarronn and he clenched his fists to contain himself. He could scent the sorceress's arousal. Mayhap he would reward her with pleasures of the flesh. Mayhap not. All would depend upon whether or not he was pleased with the choice he must now make.

For the future of his people. For the future of his kingdom.

With another growl, Jarronn swept his hand out, gesturing toward the damnable cards. "What if I order you to choose for me, sorceress?"

"I—I cannot, Milord." Kalina's fire-ice eyes remained lowered, although he imagined the caress of her brilliant amber gaze over him. Despite himself, his erection grew beneath his black breeches. "It must be your choice," she added in a near whisper.

Jarronn reached out one hand to flick the glittering heart at her left nipple. "Even if it means punishment?"

Kalina audibly caught her breath and ran her tongue along her lower lip. "Yes, Milord."

"What if I fuck one of my other servants instead of you, while you watch, to teach you a lesson in obedience?" he asked as he flicked the heart dangling from her other nipple.

"I will accept whatever punishment you deem necessary, Milord." Kalina's breast pressed toward his palm and he was sure she was eyeing his cock most hungrily. "You alone must choose your future mate."

He pinched her nipple and she held back her gasp admirably well, but Jarronn had no doubt that his sorceress enjoyed the feel of his callused fingers pulling and working the tender nub. Watching Kalina's face intently, he released the nipple and trailed his fingers down her flat belly to her bare mound. With a rough motion he cupped her and slid one finger into the delectable wetness.

The corner of his mouth curved into an almost smile as he watched her bite her lip, obviously attempting to hold back a moan. To tease Kalina's arousal, he allowed a light dose of *tigri* pheromones to flow over her.

The sorceress began to tremble. A fine sheen of sweat beaded her fair skin and her nipples grew visibly tighter. "Time is our enemy, Milord," the sorceress reminded him in a hoarse murmur. "Choose . . . *please.*"

Jarronn growled and brought his finger to her mouth.

"Taste the honey of your desire, sorceress. Your desire for your king."

Kalina parted her ruby-dark lips and gave his finger entrance to her warm mouth. She took him as though it were his cock, flicking her tongue along his finger and applying deep suction.

His erection grew mightier yet, and erotic thoughts nearly consumed him . . . of throwing the sorceress facedown on the *a'bin* amongst the cards. He would free his erection from his breeches and take her from behind, hard and fast, while he flogged her ass cheeks a hearty shade of rose. No doubt Kalina would enjoy such pleasures and would beg him for more as she always did.

All he had to do was choose a damn card.

Jarronn slid his finger from between her lips and growled again as he faced the *a'bin*.

Four cards. Four kings. Four mates.

When Jarronn finally drew the card, he knew that his emblem, that of the Ruler of the Kingdom of Hearts, would appear. His fate and the fate of his future mate would be sealed. This moment fell to him, as eldest brother and High King of Tarok.

His scowl would surely slay any who might choose to enter the sorceress's chamber at that moment, but the room remained silent save for Kalina's soft breathing. No doubt the longer he took, the more aroused the sorceress would become, waiting for whatever sexual pleasures he might treat her to. If he dared to emit more of his powerful pheromones, Kalina would become wild with need and passion. She would drop to her knees and beg.

Enough!

Never one to be indecisive, Jarronn was infuriated by his own hesitation. He had no desire for an unknown mate from one of the many other worlds, but his people were dying. Children had not been born to Tarok women for nearly two decades . . . the women were all fertile, yet none could conceive because of the damnable mind-spells of Mikaela and her legion of *bakirs*.

New hope had sprung amongst the Tarok brothers once the sorceress's cards had revealed how his people could survive and prosper. But once a Tarok male mated, he mated for life . . . and if Jarronn chose the wrong woman . . . there would be no heirs to his kingdom and little immediate hope for his people.

They would be forced to wage physical war against the Malachad Kingdom while attempting to fight off the *bakirs'* mind-war at the same time. Countless Tarok warriors would die, and Jarronn refused to waste one precious life. He would find another way to defeat the bitch Mikaela.

Flexing his biceps, Jarronn held his hand out, palm facing down, and slowly swept it over the cards. The intricate geometric design upon the back of the first one glimmered, and the card vibrated against the *a'bin's* glowing surface.

"Yes, Milord," the sorceress whispered from behind him, the timbre of her voice rich with passion. "Take it."

This time without hesitation, Jarronn reached for the card that called to his soul, called to the most basic elements of his very nature. Heat rushed through him, hot and fierce, and the heart tattoo across his left biceps burned with inner fire as he picked up the card. The power flowing through him was beyond any that he had experienced in his lifetime.

The moment he flipped his chosen card over, Jarronn rumbled with satisfaction. *Perfect.* This woman would most certainly do . . . a woman born to be his mate. Eyes as aqua-green as a Tarok sky, long white-blond hair flowing over her shoulders, soft thighs to slide between, breasts full enough to fill his large hands, and generous lips made to slide over his cock. And most certainly he would find use for the blue satin ribbon she wore in her hair. . . .

He clasped the card in his palm and caused it to vanish, using his magic to send it to the royal vault for safekeeping.

"Come, sorceress," he ordered as he shape-shifted into his hunting form. He gave a deep, vibrating growl that caused Kalina to shiver.

Jarronn turned his ice-green eyes upon the sorceress as he added in thought-words, *I have prey to stalk.*

Alice tossed her purse onto a park bench and sank down beside it. She was somewhere in the middle of Golden Gate Park, just off one of the many paths in a secluded location. She'd absently noticed the sign several feet behind where she sat and vaguely knew where she was, but right now she really didn't give a damn.

Her muscles ached as she drank in her surroundings . . . massive eucalyptus, cypress and pines, soft grass, and wildflowers. The park was a huge forest and had often been a place of refuge for her, a place where she could work through any problem that might be bothering her.

She'd been walking for hours and caught a couple of local bus lines to make it out here. Along the way she'd gone through every range of emotion: a huge dose of self-pity; anger with herself for being so stupid as to even be with Jon in the first place; anger at Jon the asshole for using her and cheating on her.

But what had echoed over and over and over in her mind, and hurt the most, was the last thing she'd heard Jon say: *If Alice wasn't so fat, I wouldn't have to—*

Alice leaned back against the hard wood of the park bench and stared up at the leaves of the eucalyptus tree overhead. A heavy ache settled where her heart should be. She bit her lower lip hard to keep it from trembling. Jon wasn't worth one damn tear from her. After she'd caught her long-ago ex-boyfriend Steve screwing around with some girl he'd met in the apartment's laundry room, she never thought she'd trust a guy again. Then came Jon with his wicked sense of humor and boyish personality.

God, she was an idiot. She'd been so desperate for love that yet again she'd settled for an l-o-s-e-r.

Why couldn't she find a man who loved her for *her*? What was wrong with being a size 16? She felt comfortable in her own skin . . . usually. Even kept herself in pretty good shape with all the walking she did around the city instead of taking the trolley or the bus most places she went.

Well, never again would she trust her heart to any man. From now on she would be more like Alexi and fuck 'em and leave 'em.

Oddly enough, Alice realized she felt relief along with the pain.

Like a part of her had recognized long ago, and just like Alexi had said a million times, that Jon was not the right man for her.

Man? Yeah, right. As if Jon was even close to being a real *man.*

From out of nowhere a giggle burst from inside Alice and right through her lips. Birds startled in nearby pines and she sat up in her seat and clapped her hand over her mouth. But at the thought of Jon's shocked face when he saw her watching him getting it in the ass Alice sniggered again and then burst into full-scale, all-out laughter. She laughed so hard that her belly hurt and tears rolled down her face.

When she finally calmed down and had wiped away the last trace of moisture from her eyes, she couldn't help the silly, almost maniacal grin that she knew was on her face. "Just think, Alice, dear," she mumbled out loud, "today certainly can't get more interesting than it has already, now can it?"

A squirrel chattered from the bough of a cypress, and Alice took that for an agreement. With a tired sigh, she kicked off her walking shoes and wiggled her bare toes in the grass. She reached into her purse and withdrew the new tube of raspberry-scented lotion that she'd just bought at a spa shop on her way to the park. After watching Stone grease himself with her former favorite rose scent, she'd decided it was definitely time for something new.

Sweaty and tired from her long walk, Alice eased out of her jacket and tossed it onto the bench next to her. Yeah, she'd definitely had it with men. She was going to be more like her twin and just enjoy men and sex with no commitment. Hell, she might as well make her fantasy come true and have two men at once.

If she could find two men who enjoyed women on the plump side.

She glanced around to make sure she had privacy—it was starting to get late and she hadn't seen anyone on her way in here. With a quick jerk she hiked up her skirt and smoothed some of the lotion between her thighs. That was one thing Alexi never had to worry about, since she was so damn slender—her thighs never rubbed together. And since Alice's were rather full, and since she'd taken her ruined nylons off back at the apartment, her thighs were good and well chafed.

The lotion soothed her skin as she smoothed it over the soft flesh. Her fingertips brushed her panties and for a wild moment she visualized herself sliding them off and bringing herself to orgasm right here in the park.

What am I thinking?

But the desire to do just that was nearly overwhelming . . . like some force was directing her. With another quick glance around the darkening park, Alice scooted her red panties over her hips and ankles and then tucked them into the bottom of her purse.

Yeah. That's better.

She frowned at her large breasts, her cleavage clearly showing in the lace-up opening of her blouse. Her breasts all but begged her to free them from her bra.

Again that force seemed to tell her, *Do it. Do it now.*

Well, why not? Who would see? She'd be putting her jacket back on, anyway.

It was a lot harder taking off her bra, and for a moment her naked breasts were exposed to the cool air, sweat chilling on her skin, her nipples growing painfully tight. After she'd shoved her bra into her purse beside the panties, she started to pull her blouse down but stopped.

Instead, she took another quick look around and then pushed her blouse up higher over her breasts. A deliciously naughty feeling raced over her skin. She squeezed more of the raspberry lotion onto her hands and massaged it into the delicate skin of her breasts and then pinched her taut nipples. It was so relaxing and stimulating caressing herself, and all the day's stress seemed to slip away.

Damn, she was close to coming, just by playing with her breasts.

Mmmmm . . . she loved the smell of raspberries. Somehow it was even more arousing, mixed with the pine and cypress scents of the surrounding trees and the smell of the Pacific Ocean. She could almost hear waves thrusting against the shore, then sweeping out, only to pound the sand again and again.

Against her will, Alice's eyelids fluttered shut and she imagined the faceless man of her fantasies. He was always dark haired, muscular, powerful, and very dominant. Maybe that's why she didn't go for submissive men . . . because deep down she wanted to be dominated.

What an incredible feeling that would be. To feel possessed and cherished. To know she was with a man who was *all* man. A man who was in control of himself, a man who was the master of his own destiny. A man who would give her as good as she gave him, and more.

She imagined the man pushing her to her knees and forcing his erection through her lips. Maybe her wrists would be bound behind her back as he clenched his hands in her hair. And she'd take all of him, enjoying the power she held over him and his pleasure.

A faint ringing snapped Alice from her fantasy. Her cell phone. *Probably Alexi again,* she thought as she yanked her blouse down and then dug through her purse and pulled out the slim silver phone. Her sister had called three times already, just to make sure Alice was all right. During one of the calls, Alice had told her sister about that bastard Mitch, and Alexi had gone even more ballistic than she already had over Jon.

Alice checked the caller ID and, sure enough, it was Alexi. She flipped it open and pressed *on*. "I keep telling you I'm okay," she said as she ran one finger along the design of her woven bracelet.

"Hello to you, too, sis." Alexi's voice switched to her get-down-to-business tone: "Do you have any idea what time it is?"

With a shrug, Alice tugged at her skirt and covered herself, her arousal vanishing like the sun through the park's trees. "I needed to walk. And there's no way I can stay in that apartment, ever again."

"It's all taken care of." Alexi's tone held smooth satisfaction. "I'll tell you all about it when you get to my place."

Alice had to smile. No doubt Alexi had been busy terrorizing the landlady and the ex-fiancé. Maybe she should have stayed and watched. The show had probably been at least as good as the one Jon, Min, and Stone had put on.

"Now where the hell are you?" Alexi was saying. "It's getting late."

"Golden Gate Park." Alice craned her neck and her gaze found the park sign several feet behind where she was sitting, and she told Alexi exactly where she was.

"I'll take the hog for a spin and meet you there in twenty." The clink of keys sounded over the phone and then Alexi added, "We'll pick up Thai on our way back."

Alice's stomach rumbled. She hadn't eaten since breakfast. "Order chicken *panang* for me, and make it spicy."

After her sister hung up, Alice snapped the cell phone shut and dropped it into her purse. Just as she was about to slip her jacket on, she caught a flash of white out of the corner of her eye. Something low to the ground had just dashed behind the massive trunk of a eucalyptus tree.

For some odd reason she felt compelled to investigate, as though she had to know what it was. Her jacket slipped from her fingers as she stood up from the park bench. A gust of wind stirred her long blond hair about her shoulders while she walked barefoot through the grass to the tree. She braced one hand against its rough, tattered bark and peered around its trunk.

A snow-white lop-eared rabbit. The bunny had bright pink eyes and a cute little pink nose that twitched as it looked up at her.

Alice smiled. It had to be someone's pet—it definitely wasn't the wild variety. "I'll bet you're lost, aren't you, sweetie?" she murmured as she took a step forward. She hesitated and squinted . . . a white tiger?

The bunny morphed before her eyes into one of those huge rare white tigers she'd seen at a magic show in Las Vegas.

Okay, Alice, now you're hallucinating. Time to go visit the doctor . . . or better yet, a shrink.

She started to back away from the figment of her

imagination just as the ground gave out from beneath her bare feet.

Terror ripped through her as she pitched into nothingness.

Alice screamed as she tumbled through air so thick it felt like pudding. Faster and faster she dropped through the black void. She couldn't stop screaming, couldn't stop falling.

Bright light stabbed at her eyes, and then she slammed onto her back, on an unforgiving surface. Air whooshed from her lungs and pain shot through her head.

For the briefest of moments she thought she saw a massive white tiger peering down at her, but then it was gone.

Her sight dimmed in a rush until the remaining speck of light narrowed to the size of a pinhead.

Everything went dark.

CHAPTER TWO

J ARRONN CUT HIS FURIOUS FELINE GAZE FROM the motionless woman lying on her back before him. Snarling and baring his fangs, he swung his tremendous paw at Darronn, cuffing his twin's ear. *Damn you, I instructed you to be careful with the woman when you brought her through the path,* Jarronn bellowed in thought-words. *This is your future High Queen!*

With a roar, Darronn bared his own fangs and sliced a ferocious glare at Jarronn. *The maid lives,* Darronn growled. *But if you are sporting for a fight, I will gladly oblige you, brother.* Fluid muscle rippled beneath his glossy striped coat and his muscles bunched as though he prepared to spring.

Slowly Jarronn turned to face the white tiger so that they were eye to eye, nose to nose, whisker to whisker. He could scent Darronn's fury, could see the barely controlled rage in the beast's green eyes.

"What do you wish for me to do, Milord?" Kalina

interrupted from behind them, a trace of amusement in her voice. She had oft seen all four brothers clash as men with their fists, or as tigers using claws and teeth, for no greater reason than the thrill and challenge of a good fight.

The High King swung his predator's gaze to the sorceress. *Fetch Karn and Ty. I will begin introducing the future queen to our ways the moment she awakens.*

"Yes, Milord." Kalina's fiery amber eyes met his briefly, and he read the pleasure and anticipation in her expression. "I will return at once with your brothers." She lowered her gaze, a hint of a smile upon her full lips, her nipples standing out hard and erect, allowing the hearts to dangle freely from them.

See that you hurry, sorceress, Jarronn ordered, and gave a low rumble. *And I shall see that you enjoy your part in this demonstration.*

The sorceress bowed and returned to the castle, her black hair brushing her naked hips as she strode away. The glittering silver chain attached to her collar dangled from beneath her hair, down her back. Yes . . . most certainly Kalina would enjoy showing the future queen what pleasures were to be had in this kingdom.

The High King's rumble turned into an untamed purr as he lowered his gaze back to the unconscious woman at his feet. Her white-blond hair splayed across the grass like a veil of fine silk that glistened in the spring sunshine. Dark lashes rested in half-moons against her pale cheeks, and her full pink lips pursed together in a small pout.

A fierce desire to protect this maid gripped Jarronn, unlike anything he'd known before, and his gut clenched. The tightening in his chest felt as if chains bound his heart as thoroughly as he intended to bind this woman to him.

The wench is beautiful, Darronn said in thought-words from beside him. *She shall be most enjoyable to train.*

Jarronn bit back the rush of possessiveness that flooded him at Darronn's statement. As if Jarronn alone would touch this woman's soft skin and feel the warmth of her beautiful curves pressed tight against his length. But that was not the way of Tarok, in any of the four kingdoms.

This wench you speak of is your future High Queen, Jarronn reminded his twin. But Jarronn's loins tightened and the thrill of anticipation raced through his veins as he thought of the pleasures he and his brothers would give this woman together during the mind-bond. *Go to the fountain and prepare to initiate my prize.*

Darronn snarled, his green eyes flaring with temper at being ordered about like a mere servant. With another growl he turned toward the gardens, his tail twitching as he stalked away.

Jarronn dismissed his brother's anger and turned back to the maid. Her gentle breathing and the strong beat of her heart met his ears. Above them birds sang from the boughs of the *ch'tok* tree, and the fountain gurgled and splashed on the other side of the slight rise.

The king padded around the woman, even as his keen senses remained aware of all that surrounded him. He sniffed at her clothing, which would most definitely have to go. Never would he stand for anything but the finest sheer fabrics to drape his future queen's voluptuous form—if anything at all.

Another possessive rumble rose up in his throat as he nuzzled the curve of her breasts exposed in the opening of her tunic. She smelled of raspberries and feminine warmth, and it was all he could do to rein in his lust. He could shift back into his man's form and take this woman hard and fast the moment she woke. She would know only pleasure and he could easily ensure she would beg him for more.

However, as High King, he would never allow himself such a lapse in control, no matter the temptation. His struggle for that control became even fiercer as he drank in her scent. With his muzzle he pushed up her skirt, exposing the soft curls of her mound. Darronn had done his job well when he'd influenced the maid to remove her undergarments. If the woman hadn't been distracted by the ringing sound of that voice-box she had spoken into, Darronn very well could have had all her clothes off before she came to Tarok.

Jarronn's nose touched her mound and he inhaled deeply.

One taste.

He allowed himself the luxury of a single stroke of his wide tongue along her slit. His rumble became a deep purr as he gloried in her sweet flavor, and in the soft moan she gave as she parted her thighs and lifted her hips, begging for more even in her sleep.

Jarronn's ears pricked toward the rainbow gardens. His three brothers and the sorceress had arrived at the fountain, prepared to treat his future bride to a view of his kingdom's pleasures.

Lowering his head, the king nudged up the soft material covering her breasts and freed both rosy nipples. With a swipe of his rough tongue, he licked one bud, bringing it to a tight peak. The woman sighed and arched her back, thrusting her chest toward him. He laved her other nipple, determined to awaken his future bride in a way that would have her senses on fire.

It is time.

He rumbled his satisfaction as she moaned again. The woman would be perfect.

So long as she obeyed and submitted to his every demand.

And providing she passed the tests that would allow her to become his queen.

This time the fantasy of the faceless dark-haired man was more intense than it had ever been. Alice could almost feel his mouth on her pussy and then harsh strokes of his tongue against her nipples. Almost as rough as sandpaper, a feeling that made it even more stimulating and exciting. The ache in her increased and she needed to come so badly she could almost scream.

Abruptly the sensation stopped. Alice became aware of a gentle breeze across her wet nipples and sunshine warming her face. In the distance she heard the splash of water and from above twitters of countless birds and the sound of wind stirring thousands of tree leaves. She blinked, her thoughts somehow foggy and confused as she found herself looking up at the branches of a blue feathery-leafed tree instead of the cracked and stained plaster ceiling of her apartment.

Turquoise sky and flashes of early-morning sunlight peeked through the leaves as a breeze rippled through.

Alice frowned.

What the hell? The last thing she remembered was sitting in Golden Gate Park on a bench. She scowled as she remembered why she'd been on that bench. That bastard Jon had screwed around on her.

Just like Steve had.

It had been late evening, and Alexi was on her way down to the park on her motorcycle. They'd planned to pick up Thai food on the way back to Alexi's apartment.

But after hanging up with her twin, Alice had seen a flash of white. She'd left everything on the park bench and followed that rabbit around the tree . . . and the rabbit turned into a white tiger—

Alice sat up so fast that her head spun and she thought she was going to hurl. She clapped her hands to her forehead, trying to still the motion of the trees and sky and flowers as everything seemed to swirl around her. For several moments she could only sit there, holding her head, waiting for the dizziness to pass.

Flashes of memories came to her as she pressed her fists to her temples. Not memories, but a dream. Yes, a dream. Ground giving out beneath her feet . . . then falling through something as thick and dark as chocolate pudding . . . slamming onto the ground . . . and a white tiger . . .

A gust of wind brushed over Alice's skin, caressing her breasts and pussy as if she had nothing covering them. She chanced a look and saw that her blouse was up over her breasts and her skirt hiked around her waist—and she didn't have on her panties and bra.

"Oh, my god." Alice scrambled to her feet, tugging down her blouse and skirt. Her cheeks burned like crazy when she remembered taking her underwear off in the park. What in the hell had she been thinking?

Another wave of dizziness swept over her and she braced her hand against the smooth, glossy trunk of the tree she was under.

When she could finally focus without feeling as though she'd pass out, her gaze moved over her surroundings. It was like no place she remembered ever seeing before. The sky was a brilliant turquoise, the clouds a vivid blue on the tops, shading down into a deep green on the bottoms. The trees around her were unusual, varieties she wasn't familiar with—and the one she'd been sleeping under had feathery blue leaves.

Flowers grew in every color of the rainbow . . . some shaped like stars and bells and others with heart-shaped petals. The air smelled unbelievably clean and fresh, so much so that the flowers' perfume and the rich forest smells almost overwhelmed her.

It all seemed surreal . . . as though she'd tumbled down a rabbit hole and landed in Wonderland.

Oh, sure, Alice. And then next thing you know the Cheshire Cat will be hunting you down. You're dreaming. Just relax and enjoy it.

A woman's moan floated along the breeze and Alice stilled.

Okaaaay . . . the last time she'd heard a sound like that she'd found the beautiful Min fucking her ex-fiancé, who was then fucked by Stone.

The deep rumble of a man's voice came next. "Draw," he said, and Alice's heart began to pound. As though in a trance, she moved toward the sounds. They came from the other side of the massive tree she'd woken beneath.

Alice pressed close to the glossy trunk and peered around it. Her skin flushed with instant heat and arousal.

Before a gurgling fountain were three incredibly gorgeous and very *naked* men. A black-haired man with scars on his chest and a diamond tattoo wielded a leather flogger in one hand as he tucked away three playing cards with his other. But where did he put them? He was naked for cripes sake.

A blond with a club tattoo and an amused twinkle in his blue eyes reclined on the lush grass. The third man, a dark-haired rogue with a feral look in his green gaze, practically growled as he stood by with his arms folded across his chest. A large black spade with flowing lines around the design was tattooed on his thick wrist, somehow making him look all the more dangerous, like a naked pirate stranded ashore.

"Ty won the draw," the man with the flogger said in a rich accent that sounded European. The blond grinned and the man with the spade tattoo most definitely growled this time.

In the midst of the men stood a beautiful naked woman with long shimmering black hair that reached the base of her spine. She wore a red leather collar and sparkling red hearts dangled from her nipples. Her head was bowed in a position of subservience and she'd clasped her hands behind her back.

They were all just feet away from Alice, so close she swore she could smell testosterone coming off the powerful muscled bodies of the men, along with the woman's honeysuckle perfume. The men were all barbarians in appearance—long hair loose about their shoulders, sculpted bronzed bodies, and fierce, almost feline expressions.

All three men had erect cocks, all impressive and much thicker and longer than anything Alice had viewed before. Hell, bigger than the biggest dildo she'd ever seen.

Alice was mesmerized. She couldn't have moved away if she'd tried. Just the thought of experiencing the feel of those cocks inside her made Alice's insides tingle.

"Kneel, Kalina," the black-haired man ordered the dark beauty as he snapped his flogger in the air. "Beside Ty." He gestured with the flogger to the blond with the satisfied smirk, who was still kicking back on the grassy slope. "I wish for you to fuck him."

"Yes, Master Karn," the woman called Kalina responded, her accent as beautiful and unusual as Karn's. She gracefully lowered herself to her knees, keeping her eyes downcast. Her hands—they were actually bound behind her back by metal bracelets attached to a chain. A chain that glittered beneath her long black hair as it trailed up to the back of her neck.

The chain was attached to her red leather collar. *Kalina must be the man's slave,* though the expression of ecstasy on the woman's face suggested she had chosen the role. She looked positively enraptured.

Alice caught her breath as Karn slowly walked around the woman, trailing his flogger over her breasts and then around her shoulders. The pounding in Alice's heart reached San Francisco earthquake proportions. She was watching a Dom and his sub . . . and he was going to share her with other men.

Oh. My. God.

What would it be like to be in the woman's position—bound, subservient, and dominated by such a powerful man? The thought was exciting and somehow freeing, and Alice was amazed at how turned on she was by picturing herself in Kalina's place.

When Alice had first heard about BDSM from her aunt Awai, she'd been horrified at first, then intrigued. The more Alice had read about it on the Internet, the more she'd been fascinated by the idea of being dominated. But she'd never been able to talk to Jon about it—he would always tell her no when she'd ask something like, *Would it turn you on to spank me when we have sex? Wouldn't it be fun if you tied my wrists and ankles to the bedposts?*

And no wonder he hadn't been interested in tying her up. *He* had wanted to be dominated, too.

Alice pressed closer to the tree, trying to control her breathing as she watched the man tease his sub. What if they caught Alice watching them? What if they wanted to punish her for spying . . . and use that leather flogger on her?

The excitement that raced through Alice's body at the thought of being punished by these men was so great that it took her completely by surprise. She swallowed and licked her lips and had to struggle to keep from slipping her finger under her skirt and stroking her clit as she watched.

"Straddle Ty." Karn lashed Kalina's ass cheeks with the leather straps.

Alice flinched, but the woman arched her back and moaned.

"Faster, wench," Karn demanded, and flogged her again.

"Yes, Master Karn." Even with her hands bound behind her back, Kalina easily straddled the blond's tapered hips with the grace of a dancer.

Ty reclined in the grass with his hands behind his head, the muscles of his arms clearly defined. Alice shivered at the thought of grasping his muscles and feeling the power in those biceps and triceps.

"Rub yourself along his cock." Karn lashed Kalina's ass with the flogger, leaving bright pink trails across each cheek. "And do not climax without my permission."

"Yes, Master." Kalina gasped, and thrust her breasts up as she rubbed herself along Ty's erection. The red hearts sparkled at her erect nipples with every movement she made. Her lips parted and her skin flushed with arousal.

Karn knelt behind Kalina and lightly ran the flogger over her back. "Suck Darronn's cock."

With that, the third man strode forward and grasped Kalina's hair in one massive hand. None too gently he yanked her head up and thrust his erection through her parted lips.

Kalina moaned as Darronn fucked her mouth and Karn flogged her ass again.

"Ty will reward you for your good behavior in this demonstration by fucking you," Karn said. "And I am going to take you in your tight ass."

Alice's hand covered her mouth as she fought back her own moan of excitement while she watched Ty hold Kalina's hips and thrust his erection into her pussy. The woman moaned around her mouthful of Darronn's cock.

Karn was stroking his own erection and it glistened as though he'd magically come up with some kind of lubricant. In the next moment he grabbed Kalina's ass cheeks and placed his cock at her anus, slowly penetrated her, and then began pumping in and out.

"Very good," Karn said in a virtual purr as he went back to flogging her ass and her back, never hitting the same spot twice. "Take us all as deep as you can."

Three cocks thrust in and out of Kalina, three powerful men taking her at once.

And more than anything, Alice wanted what Kalina was getting.

Just as Alice thought she couldn't take any more, a vibrant scent met her nose. Her body began to tremble violently. Her nipples tightened until they ached. *Oh, my god,* she had to get fucked and she had to get fucked *now.*

And then she realized Kalina was going crazy.

The woman's calm mask of serenity vanished. She made guttural sounds as she sucked Darronn's cock. He'd pulled her head back so that her brilliant amber eyes were focused on him.

Kalina's body trembled violently as Ty and Karn slid in and out of her pussy and her ass. If the men didn't have Kalina so fiercely in their control and if her hands weren't so tightly bound behind her and to her collar, Alice was sure the woman would have gone wild on them. That wildness was evident in her amber eyes, in the shaking of her body, in the way she thrashed with every thrust of their cocks and the moans rolling out from her throat and around Darronn's cock.

The primal urges welling up inside Alice frightened her with their intensity. She wanted to rip off her blouse, yank off her skirt, and join the sexual frenzy. She'd never been so turned on.

Gentle prickling erupted in her consciousness, like someone was watching her. It took effort, but she forced her gaze away from the erotic scene before her . . . and almost forgot to breathe when she saw him.

A powerfully built man rested one hip against the massive trunk of a scallop-leaved tree on the other side of the foursome. He was naked, too—only the red scarf he held in one hand draped across his thighs and hid the one attribute she was most dying to get a look at. And those thighs—good lord but those had to be the most athletic thighs she'd ever had the pleasure of viewing. His sculpted body was sheer perfection, his clearly defined abs surely as hard as carved stone.

The tattoo of a heart design flexed across one arm as his gaze focused on something he held—it looked like a playing card, only the pattern on its back *glowed*. While he studied the card, a feral smile curved the corner of his mouth. He had a light mustache and beard that made him even more devilishly handsome.

Strange sensations washed over Alice in waves that raised the hair at her nape . . . as if the man was aware of her, even though he wasn't looking directly at her.

Heat poured through Alice's veins like molten lava. She barely glimpsed the foursome as she slipped back behind the tree, praying she was wrong and that the man hadn't noticed her.

Alice pressed her palms against the tree's glossy bark, closed her eyes tight, and shivered at the thought of the man . . . looking for her. Sounds became more acute as she braced herself against the tree and trembled, hoping she hadn't been discovered. Was that the snap of a twig above the grunts and moans from the foursome? A splash in the fountain?

Then she heard Karn shout, "You may come, wench," followed by Kalina's scream of ecstasy.

Slowly Alice moved to again peek around the tree and saw Karn withdraw his cock from Kalina's ass that was still bright pink from being flogged.

The blue satin ribbon in Alice's hair flopped into her eyes, and she pushed it away with trembling fingers. Her gaze moved to the tree where the bearded man had been standing—but he wasn't there. A queer sensation settled in her belly. Where had he gone?

Something warm and soft nudged Alice's ass and she froze. A low predator's rumble surrounded her and she began to shake so badly she thought her knees would give out. Another nudge, this time harder, to one hip as though trying to force her to turn around.

Her heart pounded in her ears, her throat so dry she couldn't even swallow. Very slowly, she turned. . . .

An enormous white tiger stood behind her, his ice-green gaze fixed on her.

Horror rose through Alice so fast that her head seemed to become as light as air.

That tiger isn't real. None of this is real, was her last coherent thought as she slipped down the tree trunk to the soft, sweet-smelling grass and faded out of consciousness.

CHAPTER THREE

THE BRUSH OF FINE SILK TEASED ALICE FROM her sleep like the caress of a lover's supple lips . . . sliding down the delicate line of her throat, over the curve of one breast and her taut nipple. She murmured and tried to move toward the sensation, but her arms and legs felt somehow weighted down. The luxurious sweep of silk over her skin continued its sweet torture, swirling over her belly and farther on.

Smells of sandalwood and spice embraced her, and something far more primal and earthy. Alice sighed with pleasure at the feel of the silk, and then disappointment when the caress moved away. A sleepy smile curved the corner of her mouth as her eyelids fluttered open.

Her smile changed to a confused frown. She was lying flat on her back in a soft bed in the middle of a dimly lit room. Golden moonlight spilled through the window just beyond the foot of the bed and a breeze stirred the sheer curtains to either side of the opening. Candles glowed all around the room, perched on tables and chests. The breeze caused the flames to flicker and cast haunting shadows upon glittering walls.

One large and very dark shadow shifted beside the bed from above Alice's range of sight. She turned her gaze from the candles, past tables and a large chair, toward the shadow. Her heart stuttered.

The bearded man—the one with the heart tattoo. Except this time only his chest was bare. He wore snug black leather pants . . . with a very obvious erection outlined behind the leather.

In a fiery rush, panic swept through Alice. "Who are—" she started to say as she tried to sit up, only to discover she couldn't budge her arms or legs. She was spread-eagled, her wrists and ankles securely tied by red silk scarves.

And she was buck naked.

Fear slammed into her as she stared up at those feral eyes. Goose bumps pebbled her skin, causing her nipples to tighten more. The man's nostrils flared as his gaze traveled in a slow perusal over her erect nipples to her mound and back again to her face. Candlelight reflected in his green eyes—eyes dark with hunger, as if she was his prey and he was about to dine upon her body.

Starting with an intense prickling at her scalp, heat burned through Alice and rolled downward toward her toes. Conflicting feelings raged within. Fury at the man for binding her and embarrassment at him viewing her naked, plump body. She wanted to hide herself from the man—to cover her wide thighs, her full hips, and the gentle swell of her tummy.

Yet the way he was looking at her . . . like he *wanted* her . . .

Just the desire in his eyes was enough to add more turmoil to her already-confused mind.

Lust.

How could she want this man who had strapped her down completely naked and placed her at his mercy?

"Time to wake," the man murmured. He had an unusual accent that she couldn't place, and the sound of his voice sent a thrill straight through her. "You have slept the day through."

Alice flicked her tongue along her lower lip and somehow managed to find her voice. "What . . . what the hell is going on?" She tried for Alexi's attorney tone but failed miserably, definitely sounding a lot more like a scared little girl. "Let me go, d-damn you."

The man raised his hand as he stepped closer. A red silk scarf appeared in his palm, like magic—a scarf similar to the one he'd held when she first watched him, like the ones binding her wrists and ankles. Slowly he trailed the cloth across one of her thighs, and she trembled. "You spied on my subjects, did you not?" he asked in a deep and resonant voice.

As hot as her face flushed, Alice was sure she must have turned redder than the scarf. No question about it, she knew he was referring to the three men and woman she'd watched by that fountain in the midst of all those unusual flowers and trees.

When she hesitated, he murmured, "Never think to lie to me, wench."

She shivered at the way he'd said "wench." Not like an insult. More like a sexy endearment.

He slid the scarf back up her belly and over her nipples. She couldn't help but watch him move the silk over her body. Her skin looked flushed in the warm candlelight, and somehow attractive. Even though she was concerned and frightened, unbelievably she was also very aroused. It was as though her deepest, darkest fantasy had come to life, and right now she was too confused to make sense of the feelings swirling through her.

"Uh . . ." The words she'd intended to speak got caught up in a moan as he teased her nipples with the silk.

With a movement so unexpected it took her breath away, the man dipped his head and laved each of her nipples. To her surprise, his tongue was rough, like a cat's, and it felt so good that Alice thought she would scream from the pleasure of it. Even as she arched her back and moaned, the man straightened and said in a low and firm voice, "Untruths and disobedience will result in punishment."

"Punishment?" Alice's eyes widened and she tore her attention from her now moist and very stimulated nipples. She swallowed hard as it finally dawned on her—he was a Dom, just like the one she'd watched by that fountain. A Dom like the one from her fantasies. Dark, virile, incredibly sexy, and in control of himself and ultimately her.

And now this guy was talking about punishing her for spying on the group.

He brought his face to hers and brushed his lips so lightly over her mouth that she trembled from the brief touch and the soft caress of his fine beard. When he rose back up she wondered if she'd imagined it. "Answer, wench," he said.

Alice had never been in such a state of embarrassment and arousal and confusion all at once. She didn't know anything about this man, yet he had her so hot that she wanted him inside her more than anything at this moment. Deep inside she knew she should be more frightened than she was, yet somehow she instinctively knew this man would never harm her, would never force her to do anything she truly didn't want to do.

Damn but she hoped her gut was right and that she wasn't just kidding herself.

She caught her breath as the man tossed the scarf across her belly. As he reached for one of her nipples, the heart tattoo on his powerful biceps flexed like a living symbol of his power. His callused fingers felt warm against the taut nub, but then he pinched her nipple, hard. Alice cried out at the brief burst of pain and then moaned at the following sensations of pleasure.

The man sniffed the air like a tiger scenting his prey and a rumble rose up from his throat. Before she had time to be even more embarrassed, the man reached for her other breast and demanded, "Answer."

"Yes." She arched her back and thrust her chest toward him as he pinched her nipple harder. "I did. I watched the three men with the woman."

"And did you enjoy it?" he asked as he moved his hand over her belly and down to her mound.

Alice squirmed, pulling against her silk bindings, her body aching so badly that moisture formed in her eyes. He cupped her mound and she gasped.

"I tire of your reluctance to respond." He slipped one finger into her. "Did you find it arousing to watch them?" A moan escaped her when he thrust his finger inside her core. "Did you wish to be the woman with three cocks to enjoy?" he added as he penetrated her with a second and third finger.

Alice's desire had grown so great that tears flowed from her eyes, dampening her pillow. "Yes, damn it!" She thrashed her head and tried to press herself tighter against his hand. "I wanted to be taken like that."

He slipped his hand from out of her core and she almost cried for real, she was so damn horny. "What is your birth name, wench?" he asked as he moved closer to her.

She glared at him and thought about refusing to answer, but when he pinched her nipple again she gasped and said, "Alice! My name is Alice O'Brien."

He gave a slow nod, as though approving of her

name. "I am Jarronn, but you may refer to me as Milord."

For a moment she just stared at him. The bastard was serious.

Something snapped inside Alice. Her dick of a boss, her cheating asshole boyfriend, and now this bullshit? She'd fucking had enough.

"Listen, you arrogant sonofabitch." Alice yanked against her bindings and practically snarled at the man who called himself Jarronn. "You can't keep me here against my will. There are laws against holding people hostage, you know. My sister, Alexi, is a lawyer and she'll sue your ass so fast—"

"Silence!" Jarronn's voice thundered through the room and the candlelight flickered as if a sudden wind had swept in. His features darkened and his eyes narrowed with fury. "You have earned your second punishment."

Oh, shit. Alice swallowed and she wished she could drop right through the bed. She'd screwed up big-time now. She should have played along until she had a chance to break free and escape.

Jarronn looked so livid she was afraid he was going to beat her. What if she'd been wrong about her instincts of being able to trust him? What if he was one of those Doms who took pleasure in thrashing the crap out of their subs? One who was into brutal pain and the humiliation of his submissive.

"Don't I get a safe word?" Alice mumbled as she shrunk away from his intimidating scowl.

His eyebrows pinched together as he glared at her. "Safe word?"

She nodded and ran the tip of her tongue along her lower lip. "You know. If I don't like whatever you do to me, I get to say the safe word and you'll stop."

This time the man's dark smile scared her twice as bad as his glare had. "No safe words are necessary in Tarok." Jarronn reached toward her and she flinched, but he merely grabbed one end of her blue hair ribbon and slowly pulled on it. "You will obey my every command, wench," he said as he slid the satin from her hair. "And you will accept and enjoy whatever punishment is dealt."

Alice's heart pounded as she stared up at her captor and realized what had once been an enjoyable fantasy had suddenly become her reality. Right now she wasn't too sure exactly how she felt about that.

Very slowly Jarronn laid the satin ribbon across her neck and dragged it over her throat. "Is that clear?" he asked in a low tone that she found frightening, yet the sound of his voice caressed her at the same time.

She dropped her gaze, unable to look into those fierce green eyes any longer. "Yes," she whispered.

"Yes . . . what?"

Choking back more tears of frustration, Alice forced out, "Yes, Milord."

Jarronn contained a rumble of satisfaction. This woman had fire and spirit and would surely make a fine queen once she was properly trained. She would need that spirit and more to help lead his people toward a prosperous future once again.

And to lead them from the storm brewing on the southern horizon.

Yet with his magic Jarronn had sensed something within the maid that troubled him greatly. This Alice did not believe in her beauty or the worth of her body, heart, and soul. She had little self-esteem, which most certainly would not do for the High Queen of Tarok.

Alice's lips trembled and more tears spilled from her aqua-green eyes. However, Jarronn sensed her need for domination, her need to be able to give freely of her body and her love with no fear of losing her heart.

This woman would need to learn to trust him completely and to follow whatever orders he might dictate, for her own safety as well as the safety of his people.

But she could not truly love him or his people if she did not first love herself.

A rumbling noise emanated from her belly and Alice turned her head away from him, as though embarrassed her body had revealed her hunger.

Captivity and hunger would serve well to begin her lessons.

"Look at me," he ordered, and was pleased when she turned her tear-reddened eyes to him at once. "Your bonds shall be loosed so that you may bathe."

"Do I smell that bad?" A glint of self-deprecating humor sparked in her gaze. "Milord."

Her eyes flared in surprise as he lowered his head

and filled his lungs with her scent. Perfume of raspberries and arousal, and her own primal heat. His cock ached so fiercely it might spear through his breeches to reach her.

"Most . . . appetizing," he murmured, and Alice audibly caught her breath.

He barely contained a smile as he straightened and called toward the darkened doorway, "Kalina."

Alice's cheeks reddened, an embarrassed look flushing across her face as the sorceress stepped from the shadows and moved beside the bed. The crystal hearts dangling from her nipples sparkled in the candlelight and the soft leather collar looked elegant at her throat.

Sparkling red powder glittered on Kalina's eyelids as she kept her gaze lowered, her hands behind her back. "What is it you require of me, Milord?"

"Free Alice and prepare her body with *tili* oils," he replied, and heard Alice's soft gasp of dismay. No doubt it did not please her to be handled by another person as though she were a child or a possession, but she must accustom herself to her body being viewed and touched by hands other than Jarronn's.

"Yes, Milord." Kalina reached for a thin jar of *tili* oil from a table beside the bed. With the grace of a dancer, she climbed onto the mattress and knelt between Alice's legs. The sorceress set aside the jar and tugged at the scarf binding one of the maid's ankles. In a smooth and sensuous movement designed to increase Alice's arousal, Kalina slowly removed the tie.

The sorceress kept her eyes lowered, focusing on the future queen's pleasure. The smell of orange blossoms filled the room when Kalina tipped the jar and poured clear oil through a tiny spout and onto her fingers. Once she set the jar down, she began working the substance over the red marks around Alice's right ankle.

While the sorceress cared for Alice, Jarronn settled himself into a chair to watch the two naked and very delectable women. It was no surprise to Jarronn that he was far more aroused by the luscious Alice than the slender sorceress.

Alice bit her lower lip as the woman's small hands caressed her ankle. Her gaze cut to Jarronn and she had the childish urge to stick her tongue out at him. Why was he doing this to her? Why did he taunt her by having a beautiful, skinny goddess remove her bonds and oil her up?

Jarronn simply braced his elbows on the chair's arms and steepled his fingers at his lips, his green eyes focused on the two of them. *Dang,* he was so flipping handsome and so masterful looking. The jerk.

Refusing to look at the bastard any longer, Alice turned her gaze back to Kalina.

With an amused glance of her amber eyes, Kalina smiled at Alice. Even though she wanted to hate the gorgeous woman, Alice couldn't help but feel warmth in her chest at the friendly gesture.

Kalina rubbed more of the orange blossom–scented oil up Alice's leg to the fleshy part of her thigh and to her hip. With a casual movement the woman's finger-tips brushed the curls protecting Alice's mound.

Alice jumped. Embarrassed heat rushed through her once again.

Oh, my god. I am getting turned on by a woman.

No way was she going to look at Jarronn and let him see it in her eyes.

Kalina gave her another smile. "Have you never been with a woman?"

"No." Alice shook her head and the heat in her face magnified. "Of course not. I'm, um, straight. I like men."

As Kalina raised one eyebrow, her eyes met Alice's even as she scooted back down the bed toward the other ankle and freed it from its silk bindings. "In Tarok it matters not if you are woman or man. We simply enjoy one another."

"What's this Tarok?" As she asked, Alice couldn't help but watch the sway of the crystal hearts dangling from Kalina's dark nipples. "Is this some kind of underground San Francisco cult? Or a BDSM club?"

"I have no knowledge of such things. B-D-S-M, or cults, or San-Fran-cees-co." Kalina pronounced the words in that strange accent as she worked the oil into Alice's other freed ankle.

Those hearts sparkled at nipples that were large and dark, like raspberries. "Alice?" Kalina paused in her movements and Alice jerked her head up to see amuse-ment in her fiery amber eyes. "Are you not listening?"

For at least the millionth time since waking up, Alice felt embarrassment prickle her skin. At this rate she'd be permanently pink and permanently embarrassed.

"I'm sorry." She swallowed. "What were you saying?"

While she massaged the oil into Alice's fleshy thigh, Kalina kept her warm gaze on Alice. "You are in the Kingdom of Hearts in the land of Tarok."

"I don't get it." Alice frowned. "Kingdom of Hearts? Land of Tarok? It sounds like an amusement park."

The woman glanced to Jarronn, as though seeking his permission to speak, and he gave one shake of his head, as in *no*.

"You will soon understand," Kalina said when she moved her gaze back to Alice.

Before Alice could respond, to insist that they explain, Kalina straddled Alice's thighs. The woman began working oil into the soft flesh of Alice's belly. When Kalina started oiling Alice's breasts and massaging them in slow, sensuous movements, she thought she was going to flip right over the edge.

As Kalina plucked Alice's nipples, she couldn't help but moan. "Do you enjoy this, touching by a woman?" Kalina asked in a sensual purr.

Alice turned her gaze away from Kalina and Jarronn both. Instead she stared at a plum-colored candle on the opposite side of the bed.

Kalina caught Alice's cheeks in her palms, lowered her face until their lips almost touched, and Alice caught her breath. Kalina's long hair fell to each side of Alice's face, like a shimmering black curtain.

The woman's breath brushed over Alice's lips, her scent pleasant, like mint and sweet tea. "You have never kissed a woman?" Kalina whispered.

Alice stilled. Everything around her seemed to fade away, like it did the times she'd been out on a first date and she knew the guy was going to kiss her. Slowly Alice shook her head and felt the whisper of Kalina's mouth across her lips.

"Mmmm. One day you must." With that Kalina released Alice, leaving her staring up at the beautiful goddess.

Kalina scooted farther up to Alice's waist and focused her attention on the scarf binding Alice's left wrist.

She was barely aware of her wrist being released and Kalina rubbing more of the oil onto her arm. The woman's blue-black hair drifted across Alice's skin, as silken as the scarf Jarronn had teased her with earlier.

As she bit her lower lip, Alice's eyes met Jarronn's. His attention was completely focused on her and not on the beautiful Kalina. He was so damn gorgeous that Alice couldn't help but wonder why he'd be interested in her, chubby Alice O'Brien, when he could most certainly have his pick of any supermodel in the world. Hell, with a body like that he could be a supermodel.

But Jarronn's hands clenched the arms of his chair so tightly his knuckles had whitened. A fierce expression was on his handsome face and she could almost imagine him roaring like a tiger reined back by a tight leash.

No matter his rigid control, Jarronn wanted her. The knowledge settled over Alice like a fine cloak. It was in-credible . . . a feeling of empowerment like nothing she'd ever experienced before.

CHAPTER FOUR

WHILE KALINA UNTIED ALICE'S LAST BINDING, Jarronn's muscles tensed and he pushed himself out of his chair. He flexed his hands, fighting back his lust for his future queen before that lust took control of him.

Turning his back on the two women, Jarronn strode to the long stone table beneath the open window. Moonlight and candle flame illuminated the items he had laid there earlier. The servant's collar with its silver chain, and the nipple rings with crystal hearts . . . items to ensure the maid realized she was his to command, his to control.

For a long moment he looked out the window of Alice's warded quarters to his darkened kingdom. Warm light glowed from cottages below the castle and torches flickered from sentry posts along the curtain wall protecting his people.

In the distance he heard the rush and roar of the

Tarok River and the night sounds of an owl, a wolf's howl, and a large cat's scream as it took down its prey. Jarronn scented wood fires burning in his subjects' homes, the river teeming with fish, wildlife in the forest surrounding his lands, and the many varieties of flowers in his well-tended gardens.

A golden moon played over the land, the crops, the fields of grain. And closer, over the royal rainbow gardens and the glittering white castle walls.

With so calm and beautiful an evening it was difficult to believe that after centuries of prosperity his people were in danger of extinction.

In danger from that bitch to the south.

Jarronn clenched his hand around Alice's new collar, chain, and nipple rings, so tightly they dug into the flesh of his palm. Gritting his teeth, he forced back his anger, turned, and strode back to the women who were now standing beside the bed, waiting for him.

Kalina's eyes were lowered, her hands behind her back, her stance wide, in the proper position. Alice, however, was watching him with her chin raised high and a defiant gleam in her aqua-green eyes.

Yes, the lovely wench would make a fine queen one day. He was certain she would be a most enjoyable mate.

When he stood before her, he kept his features expressionless and merely studied her without blinking. He held Alice's gaze until her cheeks flushed a warm shade of rose and she broke the contact and looked down. But her hands flexed into fists at her sides, giving away her true feelings.

"The rules of Tarok are simple," he murmured, keeping his tone low and firm. "The first is that you will always treat me with absolute respect, whether in the tone of your voice or with your body's mannerisms. In my kingdom this means my subjects lower their eyes unless I have given them permission otherwise. All must keep their hands clasped behind their backs and their stance wide." He paused and then added, "You may look at me now, Alice."

For a moment she hesitated, and then she raised her gaze to his. She was so beautiful he wanted to touch her face and caress away the concern in her features.

Her training, Jarronn reminded himself. "The second rule is that you may not reach climax or bring yourself to orgasm unless I allow it. The third," he continued, "is that you shall not speak unless I have granted you permission. You may ask, but I will not always allow it."

Alice's lower lip trembled and her eyes narrowed, but she remained silent. That silence was a good start indeed.

"The fourth rule is that you will follow my orders without question." He watched the flare in her aqua-green eyes and he almost purred. "And the fifth rule . . . when in my presence and when within the castle walls, you will wear only these."

He held out his palm and watched as Alice glanced at his hand. Her eyes widened and her jaw dropped. Her gaze shot back to his, but he gave her a look that meant he would brook no argument from her.

Alice stared at the heart nipple rings and the collar

with its long, fine-linked silver chain that matched Kalina's, then cut her gaze to that arrogant, cocky sonofabitch who watched her with one eyebrow raised as if he was waiting for her to argue.

She trembled and it grated on her pride as she asked, "Permission to speak, Milord?"

He gave a single nod. "Granted."

"I am not a dog," she said through clenched teeth. *"Milord."*

The bastard smiled. "Thank the spirits you are not." He gestured toward a pair of silver bracelets lying on the table. The bracelets reflected the warm glow of candlelight yet appeared cold and unforgiving. They were actually manacles like the ones Kalina had worn when the men had taken her.

"If you do not wish to add those to your wardrobe," Jarronn said in a tone as deadly as the sharp edge of a knife, "you will clasp your hands behind your back and widen your stance. Now."

Alice glared at him, her lower lip trembling and angry tears pricking at the back of her eyes. She wanted to tell him to shove the collar and its chain up his finely muscled ass, and those stupid nipple rings, too. Hell, she wanted to jam them all up there herself. The silver leash glittered as it dangled over his palm, reminding her of who had the power at this moment, and it held her back as if she were a dog barking at the end of her chain.

A muscle twitched in Jarronn's jaw, and Alice knew this was a battle she wasn't going to win—at least not yet. Raising her chin, she moved her hands behind her back and clasped them together so tightly her fingers ached. In a last bit of rebellion, she flipped him the bird. He couldn't see, but it made her feel a little better.

Jarronn gave a nod of approval. "Always thrust out your chest when you are looking at me, so that I might better view your beautiful treasures."

She bit the inside of her cheek. She had to get out of this loony bin soon, even if he was sexy enough to make her damn near orgasm with just a look from those icy green eyes.

He glanced toward the manacles and Alice arched her back.

"Lovely," he murmured as he raised his hand and caressed one of her large breasts.

A moan threatened to spill from her lips, and she had to struggle to keep it back. His touch was so firm and his fingers rough and callused. Everything about the way he touched her was completely sensual. He retrieved one of the red crystal hearts and Alice caught her breath as he dipped his head and laved her nipple with his rough tongue.

Jarronn rose up and gently forced the ring over her hardened nipple, and Alice almost let loose with a groan. It felt snug, and damn if it didn't turn her on even more.

He repeated the same motions with her other side, caressing her breast and licking her nipple, and then slipping the second ring on.

The lust spiraling through Alice almost wiped out all thought of anything else. But not quite. *I've been kidnapped—but god, it's like somebody kidnapped me and threw me in my wildest fantasy. He's an ass, but I want him. Why? What the hell's wrong with me?*

Kalina remained silent beside them, but Alice thought she caught the woman watching them from beneath her eyelids.

Jarronn reached toward her with the red collar. When his hands slid the leather around her neck her gaze met his and she saw fierce desire raging in his ice-green eyes. Fiery heat roared through her as his bare chest brushed her erect nipples, causing the heart dangles to swing against her breasts. His leather pants rubbed up against her, and the hard length of his erection branded her.

Alice was certain even her heart had stopped beating. For that one moment she couldn't think, couldn't breathe. Nothing seemed to matter now but the feel of his strong hands fastening the collar at her throat, his masculine scent of wind and sandalwood, and the heat emanating from him and burning into her as his body pressed against hers.

As he finished with the collar, the fine silver chain slid down between her shoulder blades. Jarronn brushed his lips over her forehead and stepped back. "You are mine, Alice. Welcome to the Kingdom of Hearts."

Alice could only stare at him as he reached toward the bed and picked up his crimson silk scarf and her pale blue satin ribbon. He closed his hand over the strips of cloth, the blue and red ends hanging out to either side of his fist like waterfalls of fire and ice—and then the scarf and ribbon simply vanished.

No sleight of hand, no stuffing them up his sleeve or in his pant pocket. They just flat out disappeared.

Jarronn shifted his gaze to Kalina. "Bring her to the pools." And with that he turned and strode toward the doorway.

Alice watched him leave, his black hair brushing his shoulders, his broad and naked back flexing with power as he headed out of the room. The sound of his boot steps grew fainter until Alice heard nothing but Kalina's gentle breathing and the chirrup of insects from outside the window. The room seemed somehow empty without Jarronn's presence, and even with the other woman there Alice felt suddenly alone.

The truth of what was happening to her settled over her shoulders like a heavy yoke. Falling through that chocolate pudding . . . waking up in a strange and bizarre world . . . and all that had transpired between her, Jarronn, and Kalina . . .

"I'm not in San Francisco anymore, am I?" Alice said as she turned to look at Kalina, who raised her amber eyes to meet Alice's gaze. "I don't think I'm even on Earth any longer."

Kalina smiled and took both of Alice's hands in hers. "You are correct. But it is not for me to say anything further." She kept hold of one of Alice's hands and led her over the cool marble floor toward the doorway. "It is for the king to tell."

Alice was so overwhelmed at just the thought of being on another world that she almost missed Kalina's last statement. "King?" she asked as they stepped into a hallway lit with soft golden light provided by large candles in brackets along the walls. "I'm going to meet the king?"

Kalina laughed, the sound sweet and musical. "You have met him and wear his collar."

"Jarronn is king?" Alice tried to stop and almost stumbled as Kalina continued to lead her forward. "I've been felt up and put into slavery by the king of this place?"

A slight frown marred Kalina's lovely features as she shook her head. "There are no slaves in the Kingdom of Hearts, or in any one of the four kingdoms of Tarok. In Malachad to the south, yes, the evil Mikaela does keep slaves. But in Tarok, never."

"Then why the collar?" Alice touched the buttery soft leather with her free hand as she spoke and felt the cool chain sliding across her hips while they walked. "And why all the rules?"

"Are there not rules in your world?" Kalina cocked one elegant eyebrow as she glanced at Alice. "Are you not required to follow the direction of your nobles and your king without question? Are you not punished if you do not obey?"

It was Alice's turn to frown. "I live in the U.S. We don't have nobles and kings, but we have other kinds of rulers." She waved her free hand as she spoke. "And we certainly do have laws and regulations. Hundreds of them. But we're allowed to vote on the laws and can question them and work to have them changed if we feel strongly enough about it."

A sly smile curved Kalina's full lips. "Must you obey these laws as long as they exist?"

Alice's frown deepened. "Well, yes."

"And are you not punished if you break these laws?" Kalina asked as she led Alice down a short flight of marble steps.

"Yeah." Alice shook her head in exasperation. "But we're not forced to walk around naked with a collar and nipple rings for cripes sake."

Kalina shrugged. "Our worlds each function as they are meant to."

With a sigh Alice rolled her eyes to the carved marble ceiling and then looked ahead toward the end of the darkened hallway. Was there any use in arguing the point? It was absolutely crazy, but she'd fallen into some kind of hole and landed in an erotic BDSM world. Right now she was hungry and confused and so aroused she couldn't think straight, much less debate the merits or shortcomings of either world's laws.

Not to mention she was walking through a castle totally naked with dangly hearts hanging off her boobs. She thought about being traumatized, but mostly she was frustrated and pissed off—and more than a little excited. She had no doubt she'd escape. After all, she was Alexi's sister, so her soul thrived on challenge, at least at some level. And alternate universe or not, Alexi would no doubt be suing the universe itself to get her back by now.

Before she left, though, she was going to have to sample what this Kingdom of Hearts had to offer.

Trying to distract herself, Alice studied her surroundings. Through arches along the hallway she saw glimpses of massive rooms and beautiful furnishings, all illuminated by the warm glow of candlelight—thousands of candles must have been burning there. The castle smelled of roses and wood oils and the light scent of all those candles.

"If you don't mind me asking," Alice asked as they walked down another set of stairs, "what was it like to, well, to be with those three men at once?"

Kalina gave Alice a sensual smile that told her even more than her words. "To be taken by three Tarok kings at once is the most pleasurable of all pleasures. But four . . . would be like leaving this world for the golden lands."

Good lord. Alice nearly groaned aloud at the memory of Kalina taking three men at the same time. Again she belatedly caught the rest of what the woman had said. "Are you saying that all three of those men are kings?"

"Yes." Kalina brushed strands of dark hair from her face and her amber eyes looked positively rapturous. "There are four brothers who rule the four kingdoms of Tarok. Jarronn is the High King."

Wow. Somehow it was even more arousing to know that the High King had been turned on by plump Alice O'Brien. Was that true? Or had it been her oversexed imagination wanting it to be so?

A rumbling sound, like a waterfall, met Alice's ears, drawing her attention as Kalina led her through an archway. She pushed aside thoughts of Tarok's gorgeous kings as she and Kalina walked onto a wide stone path and into an exotic jungle kissed by bright golden moonlight. Alice breathed out a sound of admiration and wonder as her gaze traveled over lush palmlike trees waving in a warm, moist, and gentle wind. The breeze caught their hair, and one of Kalina's locks brushed across Alice's breast, then fell back away.

Alice felt exhilarated and wanton, her well-oiled and orange blossom–scented flesh caressed by the air, her long blond hair brushing the tops of her breasts, and the hearts dangling from her nipples. Kalina's palm was soft in Alice's, and it surprised her how comfortable it felt holding the beautiful woman's hand.

Their bare feet padded softly over the flagstone path as they neared a series of large tiered pools carved into rock. The waterfall Alice had heard when they entered the jungle fed into the topmost pool, which in turn spilled into the three pools below it.

Smells of water, along with tropical scents of orchids and rich, moist earth, filled Alice's senses. "This is just amazing," she murmured.

When they reached the bottommost pool, they stepped onto soft grass and then Kalina released Alice's hand. It was dark in this place, yet the moonlight made everything easy to see.

A monkey's shriek echoed throughout the jungle, followed by the rumbling growl of a large predator, like the tigers Alice had seen in Las Vegas. She shivered and her gaze cut to Kalina.

The woman didn't appear frightened at all. Just the

opposite, in fact. Her chin was tilted up, her chest thrust forward and rising with the strength of her breathing. A fine layer of perspiration shimmered on her fair skin, and her kohl-lined eyes were heavy lidded with arousal as she gazed into the jungle.

Alice followed Kalina's gaze and sucked in her breath, ready to let loose with a scream.

A white tiger was walking toward them, its icy green eyes focused on Alice.

Only the feel of Kalina's hand clasping her forearm and the woman's reassuring murmur of, "Watch him, Alice," kept Alice from yelling her head off in terror.

Him. Kalina had called the big, scary monster of a cat "him" like he was the prime minister or a king.

The beast's glossy white-and-black-striped coat rippled beneath the moonlight as every smooth step brought him closer. His movements were fluid and almost sensuous, and so beautiful he was absolutely breathtaking. As he neared them, Alice noticed the stripe on his upper left leg was actually in a familiar shape. It looked like the heart tattoo on Jarronn's left biceps.

And then all of a sudden the tiger was growing— changing, *morphing*, right before Alice's eyes.

It happened so fast Alice didn't know whether to scream or cry out in amazement or faint. One minute she'd been looking at a tiger, and in the next she was face-to-face with Jarronn.

If she'd needed any more convincing that she wasn't on Earth any longer, seeing Jarronn transform from a white tiger to a man sure did the trick.

"I don't believe it," she whispered as she turned her gaze up to his ice-green eyes. "You're a transformer, or—or animorph, or shape-shifter."

"I am your king." He gave her a hard, piercing look. "And you are already forgetting the rules. Must we add a third punishment?"

Heat flushed Alice's cheeks and she placed her hands behind her back as she moved her feet farther apart and dropped her gaze—only to see that he was naked. And his erection was just as long and thick and delicious looking as his brothers' had been.

"Do you wish to suck my cock?" he murmured when Alice couldn't take her gaze from his erection. "Or shall I give that pleasure to Kalina?"

Out of nowhere a hot bolt of jealousy stabbed at Alice's belly. From the corner of her eye she saw that Kalina was standing in the position of "respect" and was running her tongue along her bottom lip as though excited by the idea.

No! The intensity of the feeling shocked Alice, but she only knew that she didn't want Kalina to have Jarronn.

"I—I would like to," Alice said in a rush, and then remembered more of the BDSM stuff she'd read on the Internet. "I mean, if it would please you, Milord."

A rumble of satisfaction rose up inside Jarronn. Yes, his future queen was learning well. "Kneel, wench."

With her hands still clasped behind her back, Alice gracefully knelt before him. She visibly trembled as she stared at his erection, waiting for his command. "Suck my cock until I reach climax," he demanded.

"May I use my hands?" she asked.

He shook his head and let out a low growl. "Only your mouth."

Alice slid her soft lips around his thick girth and took him deep.

Jarronn purred his pleasure and clenched his hands in Alice's hair, pulling her head back so that he could watch her eyes. Her hair felt soft in his hand, her mouth hot and wet. He smelled her passion and knew she wanted him inside her. The scent of Kalina's desire was strong, too, and she certainly had earned many rewards for her services.

"Kalina," he said as he continued to thrust in and out of Alice's mouth. "Kneel beside Alice."

When the sorceress complied, he said, "Kalina, slip your fingers into your slit." The sorceress didn't hesitate and Alice's eyes widened. "Remember, Alice," he murmured as he held her gaze. "You may not climax without my permission."

He kept his grip on Alice's hair and his eyes locked with hers as he thrust in and out of her mouth. The need in his loins turned into a storm that raged as though it might tear him to pieces.

"Kalina, you may come," he nearly growled, and the sorceress screamed almost at once, her hips jerking hard against her hand. Birds startled from trees overhead and a monkey chattered, so loud was Kalina's cry.

Jarronn gripped the back of Alice's head and held her as his own climax thundered through him. His seed spilled into her throat as she sucked him without hesitation, drawing out every drop until he pulled his cock from her mouth.

He released her and stepped away. She licked her lips, as though savoring his taste, and stared up at him. "May I come, Milord?" Alice asked in a hoarse whisper.

"No. You have received your first punishment," Jarronn said in a low voice. "Trust me, Alice. If you learn to trust and obey me completely, without question, you will never want for release again."

Alice glared at him but said nothing. She seemed to be at war with herself, as if coming to some deeply wrought decision. At last, she looked away from him, then down at the ground. Her hands moved behind her back.

"Yes, Milord," she murmured.

Her tone clearly communicated the unspoken, *You bastard,* and the air filled with the tang of her anger and resolve.

Resolve . . . to what?

Obey him or pacify him until she got what she wanted? And did she want to fuck him or kill him?

Jarronn's lips curled with the thrill of challenge. She would submit to him or all would be lost—and she would never ever submit to a less powerful man, or any man save him. Of that he felt certain.

Surely there was no woman more perfect for him in all the universe.

CHAPTER FIVE

ALICE WANTED TO DECK JARRONN. THE BAS-
tard. She needed to climax so badly she could
scream, and he was deliberately torturing her.
He was damn lucky his cock wasn't still in her mouth or
she'd give him a little torture of her own.

Trust, my ass. What the hell does trust have to do with sex?

She bit the inside of her cheek so hard that the cop-
pery taste of blood filled her mouth. But she kept her
hands tightly clasped behind her back, her gaze lowered. She glared at his feet instead of mouthing off,
thinking how much fun it would be to slide pieces of
bamboo under his toenails.

"Kalina, your services are no longer required," Jarronn's voice rumbled. "You may return to your chambers."

"Thank you, Milord," Kalina murmured, and Alice
heard her soft footsteps as the woman walked down the
path.

Jarronn moved away from Alice. She could no longer see his feet, but she heard slight rustling noises. Was he coming up with her second punishment even now?

Heat coursed through Alice anew, and she was furious at herself for being so aroused. She was almost anxious to see what he would do to her.

What's with that, Alice?

The waterfall pounded into the highest pool, the pulsating sound somehow in tune with the throb and ache inside her. She'd been so hot and needy for an orgasm since she'd sat on that bench in Golden Gate Park. It seemed ages ago, and between watching the foursome and Jarronn's constant sexual teasing, and now this . . . Alice didn't know how much more she could take.

Or how much more she'd be forced to take.

It grew so quiet that Alice wondered if Jarronn had left her. Was this her second punishment? Being left in a jungle, alone and vulnerable, naked and on her knees? She wanted to look up, but she didn't dare. He'd made it clear she would be punished a third time if she didn't follow his damn rules.

The grass and earth felt damp and soft beneath her knees, and she was incredibly attuned to everything around her. Water tumbling from the falls and into the pools seemed louder than ever and she heard plopping sounds like fish jumping. Calls of birds, monkeys, and other creatures made the jungle feel more like a living entity than simply a place.

Gradually her anger faded and then somehow seemed unimportant, although she wasn't sure why. She thought about all that had happened and wondered at how she had ended up in this erotic wonderland. How would she get home? There had to be a way back. Alexi would be worried sick and probably running the damn police department by now. Alice missed the feel of the bracelet on her arm that she'd worn since their eighteenth birthday—Jarronn had apparently taken it along with all her clothing. Somehow the bracelet being gone widened the chasm that now separated her from her twin. Would she ever see Alexi again?

Alice forced herself to turn her thoughts to the here and now. To her nakedness and the desire raging throughout every cell in her body. All that was happening to her was just so surreal, so unbelievable. Perhaps she was asleep now and she'd actually dreamed everything. Including seeing Jarronn shape-shift from a white tiger into a man.

Could it possibly be real? Or was all of this some kind of illusion?

And that man . . . she was so incredibly attracted to Jarronn. The power in his presence, the way he made her feel just by the look in his eyes when he watched her. Predatory . . . hungry . . . *insatiable*.

Alice's memories reeled back to the moment when she'd first watched Kalina's subservience to the man by the fountain, and to how she'd imagined herself in the woman's place. It had turned Alice on to think what it would be like to give up all control to a powerful man, to be submissive to him, and to in essence be his slave.

And now here she was.

You'd better watch what you wish for, Alice.

A moist breeze stirred the hearts dangling at Alice's taut nipples and the air was warm and balmy against her bare skin. The snug leather collar felt comfortable and the cool metal of the chain lying across her back only made the throbbing within her beyond intense.

"You may stand, Alice." Jarronn's voice startled her, she'd been so deep into her thoughts and surroundings.

She very nearly looked up but managed to catch herself in time. As gracefully as she could, Alice rose to her feet, keeping her hands behind her back and her eyes lowered. Her legs tingled with the rush of blood circulating through her, and she swayed.

Jarronn's hand grasped her upper arm, steadying her and nearly shocking a cry of surprise from her at the same time. "You may look up," he said in a low and vibrant tone.

Alice tilted her head back so that her gaze met Jarronn's. His ice-green eyes focused on her in a sensual gaze that made her feel as if she was the most beautiful woman he'd ever seen. She became incredibly aware of his naked body just inches from hers. How could she want him so badly? Did any of this truly make sense?

But that power in him called to Alice, the way he mastered both himself and her. Yeah, she'd dreamed about being dominated, and about being erotically punished, too. And this man was fulfilling all those fantasies, even if he was driving her nuts by not letting her come. By not taking her fast and hard and fucking her senseless.

Jarronn brought up one hand, and she had no inclination to flinch. Even when he raised a red leather flogger to her eye level, she wasn't afraid. Very slowly, and very gently, he brushed the leather straps over her cheek in a whisper-soft movement.

Alice's heart pounded and she shivered as he continued the sensual caress, trailing the flogger over her lips and then down the curve of her neck to her breasts.

His gaze never left hers, even as the flogger teased her nipples and then moved lower toward her mound. "Do you trust me, Alice?"

She wondered at how easily the answer came to her, at why she didn't question it more. Somewhere along the line she must have lost her mind, because there was no doubt within her that at least in intimacy she could trust Jarronn. She was certain he wouldn't physically harm her—which seemed odd considering he was caressing her with a flogger for cripes sake.

"Yes, Milord," she murmured, and then trembled as he pressed the flogger against her. "I trust you."

"Trust must be absolute." He lifted the flogger away and then brought it down against her hip, just enough to sting a little and cause her to gasp in surprise—and pleasure. The heat from the swat radiated through her flesh.

"You must trust me, no matter what I might order you to do." He trailed the flogger over the skin still tingling from the lash. "Trust must be unequivocal, regardless of whether I am commanding your body or in matters of my kingdom."

Alice nodded, but yelped when he lashed her again, this time a little harder. "Yes, Milord," she said in a rush. "I trust you in anything. Everything that you might command of me."

Jarronn gave a nod of approval and stepped away, and at once she missed his presence and the warmth of his body close to hers.

"On your hands and knees," he commanded, sounding more like a king than ever.

Alice bit the inside of her cheek and winced. It was still sore from when she'd bitten it earlier. She hesitated only a second before she eased down onto the grass and she trembled at the thought of what she knew he was going to do to her. Would it hurt? Would he make her scream?

Yet even as she wondered this, her arousal magnified.

"Lower yourself so that your head and shoulders are below the level of your hips." Jarronn lightly trailed the flogger's soft leather straps over Alice's back and she shivered as she complied with his demand. Scents of grass, rich loam, and orchids filled her senses. The chain attached to her collar slid forward and pooled on the ground beside her face. As she pushed herself lower to the jungle floor, the crystal hearts dangling from her nipples pressed against her breasts.

"Very good, wench," Jarronn said in a satisfied tone. "Now widen your thighs so that I might better view your delectable quim."

Alice was sure she'd never stop blushing. Her ass

was probably bright red from the embarrassment that flushed through her body. Which would be even redder once he got through with that flogger, no doubt.

"You are exquisite," he murmured while he caressed her skin with the flogger, along her spine and down to her ass.

Alice had always thought she had a fat rear end, but right now she felt beautiful and desirable and wanton all at once. She relaxed, enjoying the sensuous movement of the soft straps as Jarronn swished them over her hips and down along each of her thighs. She couldn't help but moan.

"Do you remember why you are being punished?" Jarronn asked as he raised the leather away from her.

"Yes, Milord." Alice's voice trembled and she dug her long fingernails into the moist earth. "For disobedience."

The first lash fell across Alice's ass and she cried out. Tingles erupted over her skin, and to her surprise she enjoyed the stinging pain. In fact, it had felt kind of good, and so stimulating that she wondered if it was possible to climax just from being flogged.

Another lash fell and another over her well-oiled flesh . . . on her buttocks, her thighs, her back. Each lash seemed stronger than the last, none falling in the same location consecutively. The stinging mounted, and Alice heard herself moaning. She wanted him to flog her harder and take her at the same time. Had anything in her life ever felt like this?

Pleasure and pain joined and separated, joined and

separated. Fear rose up and died down. Trying hard to keep breathing, Alice gave herself up to the sensations, trusting Jarronn not to harm her.

The flogger fell upon her like warm rain and star-light, biting and soothing all at once, driving her into a world where fantasy and reality collided. It erupted into a blend of ecstasy and rich sensation, of desire and need.

If she could have arched into the lashes, she would have.

Pain stopped being pain, then. Only perfect fulfill-ment, release, even joy. Higher and higher she rose to-ward the peak of a climax that might surely devastate her once she tumbled over the precipice. If Jarronn only allowed her to.

"I'm close to coming, Milord," she mumbled, her body trembling with the force of her need. "Please."

The lashes stopped. The flogger settled across her hips and he knelt down beside her. He didn't even have to touch her. All it took was his command, "Come for me, Alice."

The orgasm burst through her like a conflagration of epic proportions. Flames licked along her skin, fir-ing every nerve ending in her body, burning in her loins and across her stinging, electrified skin, straight to her soul. Her core spasmed so hard that her ass cheeks clenched and unclenched over and over again.

Heat infused her head, and it was like the Fourth of July behind her eyelids the way colors burst through her mind. Tears trickled from her eyes, spilling to the damp jungle floor.

She was vaguely aware of Jarronn picking her up as if she were as light as a child and cradling her close to his chest. It seemed as though her orgasm would never stop, her womb continuing to contract as he carried her. Where, she didn't know, didn't care. She just felt safe and secure in his powerful arms.

His warm masculine scent surrounded and comforted Alice as her tears spilled onto his sculpted chest. A splash met her ears and she found herself gradually immersed in the welcoming embrace of warm water. It soothed her body and made the tingling on her back and buttocks even more pleasurable.

Jarronn held his future queen tight to his chest and studied her lovely face as he moved across the lowest pool. Her tears called to his heart and soul, and he knew that she cried not from pain but from the sheer pleasure of her release. He sensed, too, her need for domination, and that at the most primal level the pain freed her from what she perceived to be the prison of her flesh.

He eased them both into the alcove and onto a seat fashioned from a shelf beneath the second pool. They were still in the warm waters of the lowest pool, but behind the small curtain of water that fed from the one above. He used his magic to cause a gentle glow to emanate from the rocks behind them, so that he might see his future queen better.

Cradling Alice's soft form in his lap, he kissed each

of her eyelids, flicking his tongue over her wet lashes and tasting the salt of her tears until she no longer cried. He raised his head and saw her tentative smile. Her brilliant aqua-green eyes opened and when she looked up at him he very nearly ceased to breathe.

Jarronn stroked her long blond tresses from her eyes. "You are lovely beyond any woman I have ever known," he whispered, and her smile dimmed. He cupped her chin and frowned. "Why do you not see your own beauty?"

Her lower lip trembled and he witnessed a thousand heart-wounds in her eyes. Anger at those who had hurt his future queen roared through him and he bit back a snarl of rage. Who dared to make his precious Alice feel as though she were anything but the beautiful, sensual woman he clearly recognized her to be?

Alice must have seen the fierceness in his eyes and thought his rage was directed at her. She swallowed, then hurried to answer. "I'm fat. I'm not slender and gorgeous like Kalina, or even my twin, Alexi."

"Shhh." Jarronn stroked his knuckles down Alice's cheek and she shuddered with obvious desire from the contact. "I do not understand," he murmured. Very slowly he began touching her body, stroking the firm flesh of her arms, caressing the swell of her generous breast, loving the feel of her soft belly, full mound, and attractive thighs beneath his callused palm. "You are so enchanting, your body so lovely, that I fail to see why you do not recognize your gifts."

Pink tinted Alice's cheeks. "Where I come from, a

woman is only considered beautiful if she's thin and has a perfect figure."

"It is clear your world is not deserving of you." He scowled at the thought of anyone treating his future queen with anything but the utmost respect and awe. "You *are* perfect," he murmured, and before she could argue he lowered his head.

Alice caught her breath as Jarronn's face neared hers. Her heart fluttered and her senses spun as his mouth hovered a whisper away. His lips came down fierce and hard, claiming her like a powerful warrior king of old claiming his virgin prize. His light beard felt soft against her lips and chin as his mouth moved over hers in a deep and sensuous kiss. Their tongues met and mated and Alice moaned at the rough feel of his catlike tongue. Jarronn purred, a primal sound that rose up in his chest and reminded her of the white tiger. Of *him.*

She couldn't believe he considered her beautiful. And how serious he seemed when he touched her and called her exquisite. Was it possible that on this world it didn't matter what size she was? Or was it Jarronn, the man, who saw her as no one had seen her before?

Need and desire spiraled through Alice, more intense than ever, and she squirmed in his lap. She became aware of his very large and hard erection pressed against her ass. She wanted him inside her, more than anything.

Jarronn apparently sensed her passion and seemed determined to torture her out of her mind. He pulled away from the kiss and his face was serious. "Promise me that you will love your body and yourself."

Alice hesitated, fighting back years of self-abuse. Years of hating the way she looked, the hateful things that had been said about her weight, and years of feeling invisible next to her slender sister. No matter how much Alice loved Alexi, it had not been easy being her twin.

The king's expression turned fierce, and Alice's eyes widened. "I—I promise, Milord."

His gaze remained fixed on hers, and she knew that he meant every single word when he said, "If you break this promise, your punishment will be far more severe than what you have been dealt thus far. Do you understand?"

She nodded, her hair sliding against the arm that held her tight. "Yes, Milord."

With a growl of approval, Jarronn carried her from behind the curtain of water and continued until he reached the middle of the moonlit pool. In an easy motion he tilted her head back so that her hair was completely wet, then set her down so that she was standing. Water trickled from her wet hair down her back and over her breasts. Fine grains of sand shifted beneath her feet and she nearly jumped out of her skin when she felt fish lightly nibbling at her toes.

Trust, she reminded herself before she opened her mouth to mention it to Jarronn. *You're supposed to trust him, Alice. He wouldn't set you down just to have something munch on your feet.*

"Assume the position," he commanded, and Alice immediately lowered her eyes, clasped her hands behind her back, moved her feet farther apart, and did her best to ignore the fish nibbling at her toes and knees.

She didn't know where he got it from, but Jarronn began washing her hair with an orange blossom–scented shampoo. For such a large and powerful man his hands were gentle as he worked the lather and massaged her scalp. "Tell me about this world you come from, Alice," he ordered as he shampooed her hair.

"What would you like to know?" she asked, and then hurriedly added, "Milord."

"Everything."

Okaaay. If that isn't a lot to ask a girl.

At first she felt a little shy, but it helped looking down at the dark water while she spoke. She wondered then if that was one reason why he demanded she keep her gaze lowered—to allow herself the freedom of no distractions, and the freedom of turning everything over to him.

Talking to Jarronn about herself became easier as he responded to what she told him, and easier yet as he asked her questions, prompting her to go on. While he shampooed and rinsed her hair, then massaged in a rich conditioner, Alice told him about growing up in San Francisco with her sister, Alexi. Alice talked about some of the mischief they'd gotten into—like the time they'd spied on their aunt Awai when the twins were thirteen and Awai was twenty-one. Awai had just gotten home from a date with a hot guy, and the girls had snuck out of the house and had watched the couple have sex in the backseat of Awai's red Mustang. Just as she shouted with her climax, she'd seen the twins peeking in the car's window. The twins had been grounded for two solid months after that bit of fun.

Alice also told him about the time they'd managed to turn their cousin Annie's butt-length hair orange in a failed experiment. It took Annie years to grow it out so that it was all a glossy dark brown again, and just as long for her to forgive the twins.

When he was finished with Alice's hair and had rinsed it clean, Jarronn began to wash her body with the same orange blossom–scented soap. With his prompting, she talked about how her dad had cheated on their mother and left them when the twins were teenagers. The bastard had just up and abandoned them, moved to Florida with his bimbette bride, and Alexi and Alice had ceased to exist as far as he was concerned. Last she heard, the dick and the bimbette had twin boys who never stopped moving or talking, and Alice hoped dick and bimbette were both bald from tearing their hair out.

Alice couldn't believe she shared with Jarronn about how her and Alexi's mother had sort of mentally faded away and became a transient once the girls left home. They didn't even know where she was right now, although it was probably somewhere warm like Southern California. Alexi and Alice had tried to give her a home, had tried to help her, but she kept vanishing and then would turn up every now and then, out of the blue.

It was the first time Alice had been able to talk

about it without crying. Why did she find it so easy to talk with Jarronn? Perhaps it was the way he seemed to listen without judging, and the note of caring in his tone with every question he asked.

It was harder to tell him about Jon and Steve, the men who had cheated on her, but when Jarronn urged her to she could do nothing but obey. He rinsed the last of the soap from her body as he listened to her, and she could feel the tension and the anger rising within him.

An ache lingered within her that wouldn't go away. She knew that it was her failings. She wasn't slender and beautiful.

Alice didn't realize she'd spoken the last part aloud until Jarronn abruptly caught her chin and forced her to look at him. She gasped at the angry light in his green eyes. "Those bastards do not deserve to breathe the same air as you," he growled. "Do not waste another thought on them."

She swallowed and whispered, "Yes, Milord."

Jarronn's mouth came down on hers in a hard and brutal kiss. He pressed his body tight against hers, his erection so rigid against her belly that she was sure it had bruised her flesh.

That feeling of empowerment rushed over her again. To know that she affected this man so strongly made her feel exhilarated. Maybe she was as beautiful as he said she was. And maybe with Jarronn as her Dom she could love her body and be happy with who she was. Just maybe.

CHAPTER SIX

HUNGER FOR HIS MATE AND ANGER AT THOSE who had hurt her drove Jarronn to ravage Alice's mouth. While his tongue plunged inside her, he gripped her buttocks, pressing her full length tight against his erection, forcing her to acknowledge what she did to him.

It took all his control not to throw her upon the pool's grassy bank and take her till she saw sense. Until she realized how beautiful and desirable she truly was.

Before he released her, Jarronn bit her lower lip, hard enough to draw blood and causing Alice to cry out. A feral rumble rose within his chest as he lapped at the spot of blood, savoring yet another of her unique flavors.

When he pulled away, Alice appeared dazed, her aqua-green eyes filled with confusion. And definitely lust.

Yes, there was no doubt she wanted him. But would

she ever love his people and his kingdom if she could not even love herself?

Damnation but he'd make her see herself for the beauty she was. And she would fall in love with him.

"You have earned your third punishment," he said softly, and watched as her eyes widened. "Already you have broken your promise to love your body and yourself." He brushed his knuckles against her cheek. "Do not make me have to punish you again for this."

"Yes, Milord," she whispered.

He took her hand in his to help her from the pool. "Come. Let us be done with it."

Alice's wet body glistened in the golden light of the moon as she walked beside him onto the grassy shore. He breathed in the rich scent of her arousal and his cock hardened even more. "You are truly a goddess," he murmured.

"I—" Alice dropped her gaze to the grass. "Thank you, Milord."

Jarronn's jaw tightened. If it was the last thing he did, he would set this maid free of her heart-wounds.

He stopped when they reached the middle of the clearing and released her hand. "You will walk behind me with your head bowed and your hands behind your back."

"Yes, Milord," Alice responded, and he turned away from her without another word.

Her heart pounded and tears threatened to rise as she followed Jarronn. She'd been through every range of emotion during the past day or so, however long it was that she'd been gone. And now after she had spent such a wonderful time with Jarronn in the pool, he was taking her to a punishment supposedly more severe than being flogged.

Why did she give in so easily to his demand that she follow him in a subservient manner? Was it just the fear of punishment? Or was it because deep down she enjoyed submitting to him?

Alice bit her lip and flinched from the pain of Jarronn's predatory and possessive bite in the pool. Maybe it was both . . . her fear of what kind of punishment he might deal and because a part of her loved being completely dominated by him.

Was that too weird? Was there something wrong with her for getting off on all this?

Even as she trailed after Jarronn with her head bowed, she couldn't help but sneak peeks at his tightly muscled ass and broad shoulders. He walked with power and purpose in his fluid stride, as though completely comfortable in his nakedness. Which, no doubt, he was.

When they reached the castle, Jarronn took her inside, but instead of returning down the hall she'd come from, he opened a small wooden door to their left. She followed him as he ducked through the door and into the darkness. A moment later a torch flickered on the wall and he started to climb up the steep, spiraling staircase inside a very high, circular room.

Her heart sank to the pit of her stomach. This wasn't good. She was in some kind of castle turret, and he was going to take her to the top and lock her away like Rapunzel.

As they trudged up the creaking staircase, torches magically lit along the way. A serious case of butterflies began bouncing around in Alice's belly. Her wet hair felt cold on her naked skin and she sneezed from the musty smell of the stairwell.

The fine chain hanging down her back from her collar seemed to weigh more heavily on her, and the hearts at her nipples felt as though someone was pulling on them as she walked. With each step she felt like a prisoner coming closer to meeting her doom.

Trust him, Alice, a voice whispered in her mind. *Trust him.*

Thanks to a lifetime of climbing up steep hills and countless staircases in San Francisco, Alice was only partially out of breath by the time they'd climbed at least ten flights. The stairs ended at a tiny landing in front of a wooden door with a silver keyhole.

This *really* wasn't good.

Jarronn produced a large silver key out of nowhere and inserted it into the hole. She didn't know what to expect, but when the door swung open and she saw the big silver ring fixed in the wooden floor at the center of the round room she almost turned and ran back down the stairs.

Instead, she swallowed back her fear and followed him inside. Torches flickered to life around the spotless room and she saw that there was one window and nothing else but the big silver ring.

He stopped beside the ring. "Kneel," he commanded.

Hoping against hope that he wasn't going to lock her up and leave her here, she kept her head bowed and obeyed. The wooden floor was smooth and hard beneath her knees as she widened her thighs and clasped her hands behind her back. Through the lone window a breeze swirled through the room and caused her damp hair to stir about her shoulders.

A rumble came from her stomach and heat rose in her cheeks.

"Do you trust that I will care for you?" Jarronn knelt in front of her and hooked his finger under her chin, raising her face so that her eyes met his. "You must ask for whatever you require."

"I trust you, Milord." Alice turned her face away from him, but he took her cheeks between his palms and forced her to look back to him. "I—I'm hungry. I haven't eaten since before I came to Tarok."

"There is no shame in asking for what you need, Alice." With his thumb he stroked a strand of damp hair from her eyes. "And certainly there is no shame in hunger."

"Yes, Milord," she whispered, unable to look away from those green eyes.

He reached around her neck and she hoped that he would kiss her again like he did after she had that incredible orgasm. That kiss had been like nothing she'd ever experienced before.

But instead he grasped the chain and brought the

end to the metal ring. With frightened fascination, she watched as he pressed the ring on her chain to the one in the floor and they melded somehow so that her chain was now hooked to the floor.

He was really going to chain her up and leave her here.

Tears burned behind her eyes and she bowed her head to avoid his gaze. A part of her wanted to rebel and scream at him. Why didn't she?

Because he'd only punish her more? Or because she wanted to please him?

Probably both.

"Look at me, Alice," he said in a firm tone.

She raised her gaze and met his.

"Do you understand why you are being punished in this manner for your disobedience?"

"Yes, Milord." Her lips trembled as she sorted through her feelings and thought of an appropriate response. "Because I disobeyed when you made me promise to love my body and myself. And you said the punishment would be far worse than being flogged."

Jarronn gave a slow nod. "I will leave you here so that you will have time to think about this, and only this. You are a beautiful woman, Alice." He raised his hand and cupped the side of her face. "Free yourself from the prison of your mind and you will be free of this room."

Her head swam with one thought battling another until she thought she'd scream.

"Turn, so that your back is to me."

Alice bit her lip to keep from crying and did as he

bade her to, the floor hurting her knees as she moved. When her back was to him, she felt something cold clasp around her wrists, and then her tears fell for real.

Oh, god. He'd just manacled her wrists together.

"Face me again."

Hot rivulets rolled down her cheeks as she moved back. She kept her face lowered and tears splashed onto the wooden floor.

"Drink this." Jarronn held out his hand and a small blue bottle appeared on his palm. "This will assuage your hunger, and allow you to think clearly about your punishment."

An absurd giggle rose up in Alice as she stared at the bottle. The strange purple lettering on the bottle probably said: *Drink Me.* Maybe when she swallowed the fluid in the bottle, like Alice in Wonderland, she'd shrink down until she was only ten inches high and then she'd slip right out of her collar and manacles. Hell, the hearts would drop right off her nipples and she'd be totally free.

But did she really want to be free of him?

"Tilt your head back," Jarronn commanded as he uncorked the bottle, and she had to struggle to keep the look of manic giddiness off her face as she raised her chin and parted her lips.

The fluid rolled over her tongue, and immediately heat spread throughout her body. The warmth started at her mouth, flowed to her scalp, and then flushed over her breasts, waist, and between her thighs, on down to her toes. The elixir tasted of berries and cream with a hint of mint mixed with a good dose of whiskey. By the time she'd swallowed every drop, she felt downright tipsy and not at all hungry any longer, and unbelievably even more aroused than she already was.

Curiouser and curiouser . . .

Alice snorted back a laugh but quickly lowered her gaze and assumed the damned position of respect.

He moved so close to her face that his erection was up close and personal.

Watch it, buddy. Might put an eye out with that thing.

With a low purr, the king grabbed Alice's hair and pulled back on it so that she was staring up at him. Damn but he looked wild and gorgeous.

"You are here for my pleasure, wench," he murmured. "I wish to enjoy some of your treats now."

She licked her lips and her pulse rate increased. "Yes, Milord."

"Lie on your back." Jarronn gestured beside her, and when she looked she saw that there was now a large, round cushion, like a giant red *papasan,* near the ring. How did he do those magical things he did?

Alice tried to be graceful but didn't even come close as she fell onto her side on the cushion. She rolled onto her back, her manacled hands trapped behind her. Fortunately, her collar chain that was attached to the ring in the floor was long enough that she didn't choke herself.

Excitement swirled within her as Jarronn straddled her waist. He was finally going to take her. He moved up so that his delicious cock was nestled between her large breasts and he purred.

"Perfection," he murmured as he grasped her breasts in his hands and pressed them tight to his erection. "I am going to fuck your lovely breasts and spill my seed upon your face, wench."

Alice shivered. "Yes, Milord."

Jarronn teased her nipples around the heart rings with his thumbs while he slid his cock between her breasts, pushing so far up that its velvety soft tip brushed against her lips. "Lick it," he instructed, and every time his erection neared her lips she flicked her tongue over its head. She tasted the salty sweetness of his essence and she moaned with pleasure at the feel of his thumbs rubbing her nipples, tugging at the heart rings, and his cock brushing her lips.

"It pleases me to have you bound and at my command." His eyes were fierce with passion and his long black hair wild about his face as he thrust his hips and moved his erection between her breasts. "It will please me even more when you are truly free, Alice."

Alice didn't question his words. She wanted him more than anything or anyone she'd ever wanted before. She couldn't move her gaze from his, watching the savage enjoyment he took from her body. To think that she was responsible for his pleasure made her even more excited.

It was an exchange of power . . . she turned all control over to him, yet she had power over his pleasure.

When he finally came, it was with a roar like a jungle beast. She licked his delicious taste from her lips as he came. A sheen of sweat glistened across his massive chest and shoulders and the smell of his musk added to her lust. The man was gorgeous beyond belief.

Alice squirmed, wanting him to take her, but instead he produced a red silk scarf and wiped away the come. When he finished, he eased off of her and knelt with his arm propped on one knee.

"Please, Milord." Alice widened her thighs, inviting him to slide between them.

"Shhh." He caressed her cheek, rubbing his thumb over her lips. "It is not about your pleasure. It is about mine. When you have pleased me by learning your lesson, then you will have earned your release."

As he rose up and then walked away she could only stare at him, trying to make sense of what he'd just said. Her lust-filled brain kept coming back with *doesn't compute*.

When Jarronn reached the door he turned back. "Do you trust me, Alice? Do you believe you will be safe by yourself in this room?"

Alice wasn't sure if it was the high the elixir had given her or the fact that she was so horny she couldn't think . . . or maybe it was that she did trust him not to leave her in an unsafe situation. Whatever it was, she found herself nodding and saying, "Yes, Milord. I trust you."

He smiled then. With a flick of a finger the torch lights went out and the room went dark save for moonlight pouring in through the window. In a low voice he said, "You are beautiful, Alice," and then he closed the door behind him.

Jarronn still ached and he longed to slide into Alice's luscious core and take her time and time again. But it was necessary for her training that she realized she would be fully punished for disobedience, including withholding her sexual release. He was certain she would be prepared to leave the turret's confines come morning. It pleased him greatly how quickly she learned and how well she was made for him.

Kalina stood upon the landing, waiting for him as he had bade her to. Earlier he had summoned the sorceress with his magic while he escorted Alice to the tower. No matter that he would ward the turret before leaving, he would never leave his future queen, or any other subject, unattended in such a manner.

"Look at me," he commanded Kalina after he locked the turret door.

The sorceress raised her eyes and he saw that her pupils were dilated, her fire-ice gaze telling him she was in need of release. No doubt she had listened. He required Kalina's full attention on his future bride and could not afford the sorceress being distracted by her lust.

"You may bring yourself to climax," he said, and watched as she slipped her fingers between her thighs and stroked her clit.

"Thank you, Milord," she murmured as she brought her free hand to her breasts and tugged at her nipple.

Jarronn smiled. It pleased him to watch the sorceress's skin flush and to smell her arousal. It would please him far more to watch Alice one day.

In moments Kalina's body shuddered as she reached climax. Jarronn nodded his approval and then warded the chamber. He used the most powerful of magics to keep that bitch Mikaela or her *bakirs* from using any mindspells against Alice while she slept. Unfortunately, it took far too much of his magic to ward a single person and he was unable to protect everyone in his kingdom.

And it was far too late for their protection as it was.

One way or another, Jarronn and his brothers must deal with Mikaela and put an end to her twisted mind-war.

With a low growl, Jarronn shifted into a tiger. *I will return and relieve you of your duty shortly.*

Kalina transformed into a tiger and took her place before the turret door. *Yes, Milord.*

He bounded down the steps from Alice and Kalina to lope to the jungle where his brothers awaited him.

It had been years before they realized that it was Mikaela and her legion of psychics, her *bakirs,* who had wrought mindspells upon the women of Tarok, making them believe they were infertile. By the time they learned of Mikaela's covert war, they had gone a Tarok decade with no new births. The mindspells were so powerful that Jarronn, his brothers, and their most powerful sorcerers and sorceresses had found no way to break them.

Or perhaps her mindspells had gone so far as to make them all believe there was no way to defeat her.

Jarronn snarled as he bolted out the castle door and toward the jungle.

Wind slid over his glossy tiger coat and moonlight illuminated his path toward the jungle behind the castle. During the spring the moon was at its brightest and fullest, as though showing off its finest plumage to entice a mate. Yet for nearly twenty years it had mattered not in Tarok, for no women had been able to conceive.

Youngest of the Tarok clan, Mikaela was not left a portion of the Tarok Kingdom. When the former High King and Queen of Tarok lay upon their deathbeds after contracting an incurable disease, they had divided the expansive kingdom into four lesser kingdoms and presented them to Jarronn, Darronn, Karn, and Ty. They left Mikaela nothing. At the time no one understood why, but perhaps their parents had seen that she was far too twisted to serve the people of Tarok. She preferred to serve herself.

Not long after their parents' deaths, Mikaela joined with Balin, King of Malachad, to the south, to become his queen.

Through Kalina's readings in recent years Jarronn and his brothers had learned that Mikaela had mind-seduced Balin. Over the years she had used her extraordinary mental gifts to take over the minds of those in the Malachad realm. She trained all with psychic powers to be *bakirs*, those who would use the powerful mindspells to invade the dreams of the women of Tarok. To render them infertile simply by making them believe it to be true.

The king was a mere figurehead now, and Mikaela ruled the country. She was consumed with hatred for her brothers and determined to have her revenge for being slighted by their parents and make all of Tarok hers.

When Jarronn reached the weretiger den in the middle of the jungle, Darronn and Ty were sparring as tigers. As usual, Ty was taunting Darronn, raising the ire of their brother who was quick to anger. Karn merely reclined against a tree in his man's form, with an amused expression on his face as he watched his brothers.

Jarronn shifted to his human body when he arrived in the clearing, and when his brothers saw him they quickly followed suit.

"Is the female prepared?" Ty asked with an eager expression as he used the back of his hand to wipe sweat from his forehead.

"She will be." Jarronn scowled at Ty as he folded his arms across his chest and then looked to Karn and Darronn. "Alice's training has only begun and already she is advancing far beyond my immediate expectations."

"We have little time to wait." Darronn spit into the grass at his feet and turned his glare to Jarronn. "Our kingdoms are vulnerable without us. We must return as soon as possible."

Jarronn emitted a low growl and clenched his fists. "Your future High Queen's safety is what you must be concerned with now."

"Jarronn is right." Karn eased away from the tree. "Once we have all bonded with the maid and have ensured her safety, we can return to our own kingdoms and seek our own mates."

"How much longer?" Ty asked, and Jarronn's scowl deepened. The whelp was far too anxious to bond with Alice, as far as Jarronn was concerned.

And to his surprise he was in no hurry to share her. "At most, ten days," Jarronn replied.

"Ten days?" Darronn shouted. "We have not that much time to waste."

"As long as it takes," Jarronn replied with barely reined fury. "You will do whatever you must to serve your future queen and your king."

After Alice heard the lock click, she rolled onto her side and closed her eyes, unable to believe Jarronn had left her, desperate again for an orgasm. Not only that, but she was manacled and chained up in the middle of a castle turret. And for cripes sake, she'd told him she felt safe!

Maybe just like the pretend Alice from the book, she'd open her eyes to find herself with her head in her sister's lap. Alexi would be brushing leaves away from her face as she said, *Wake up, Alice dear!*

Alice sighed and opened her eyes. Of course Alexi wouldn't say, *Alice dear.* No, Alexi would probably roughly shake her and say something like, *What the hell's the matter with you? Get up already!*

God but she missed her sister.

Moonlight spilled into the room, and she wondered

at how it stayed so consistent, so golden, for so long. Wasn't this world turning like Earth? Her thoughts moved across the time she'd spent so far in Jarronn's kingdom. Was it only a day? It seemed like a week already.

Maybe it was the elixir Jarronn had given her, but for some reason Alice hadn't felt like crying since she'd swallowed it. Her thoughts seemed clearer, and it was easier to analyze why he'd left her chained to a ring in the middle of a castle turret.

Boy, if that didn't sound weird. *Twilight Zone* weird.

A lesson. He wanted to teach her a lesson. Did she even want to be taught anything?

You are beautiful, Alice, he'd said before he left. He'd told her she was lovely and perfect and so many other wonderful things more times than she remembered ever hearing in her life. Oh, she'd been told she had a pretty face and that she'd be lovely if she shed a few— okay, a lot of—pounds, but she never remembered anyone saying that she was beautiful just the way she was.

But if she was honest with herself, she wasn't bad looking at all. Her eyes were her best feature—large and almond shaped and a unique shade of turquoise. She might not be slender, but she had a nice curvy shape, and she rather liked the fact that she had such large breasts. Her hair might be fine and not as wavy as Alexi's auburn locks, but Alice was a true blond and at the office she had worked with women who paid to make their hair that shade.

But beautiful . . . Alice had never allowed herself to think that way. It would be prideful or conceited to think of herself as beautiful, wouldn't it?

The moonlight coming into the room seemed brighter yet. Alice fancied dancing in those rays, nude, and not caring who saw her—maybe with Jarronn and his brothers all watching—perhaps reveling in the fact that the men enjoyed her body and found the sight of her nakedness arousing.

A wild sensation skittered through her body. What if she was beautiful, at least according to any standards on any planet in the galaxy other than her own? After all, wasn't Rubenesque in before Twiggy and supermodels came along?

Say it, a voice seemed to say in her mind. Was it her own? *Say it out loud.*

"I am—" Her words locked in her throat. She couldn't. *Yes, you can.*

Alice swallowed and thought of herself the way Jarronn saw her. The appreciation in his gaze as he caressed her with the scarf, when he'd trailed the flogger over her skin, and when he'd bathed her in the pool. His words, his touch, the look in his eyes—it was incredible, unlike anything she'd ever known before.

Say it, the voice repeated.

"I am beautiful," Alice whispered. A tingling started at her nape and for a moment she just sat there. In a much louder voice, with more purpose behind it, she said, "I *am* beautiful!"

Saying that one statement aloud was—was *powerful*. *Freeing.*

She said it again, and yet again as she pictured herself as she truly was, not through the eyes of people on fat-hating Earth. It might have been minutes that it took to realize the truth, or it could have been hours. What freed her might have been what she saw in Jarronn's eyes. It might have been what she'd known all along. Hell, it could have been the elixir that made it all so crystal.

Whatever the case, it rang clear to her heart. It was like a weight had been lifted off her shoulders. The weight of years of self- and peer abuse over her image. She was beautiful, damn it.

A warm feeling embraced her and she smiled. It didn't matter anymore that she was manacled and chained. What was important was that for the first time in her life Alice O'Brien could conceive of loving herself as much as she'd always wanted to be loved by everyone else.

CHAPTER SEVEN

IT WAS EARLY MORNING WHEN JARRONN AWOKE AT the foot of the turret door where he was curled up in his tiger form. Even as he had slept, his mind remained conscious of Alice. He had felt her struggle as she worked through her lesson. And his heart had known great joy when he sensed her acceptance and the freeing of her mind, heart, and soul that came with it.

The elixir had aided in her progress, yes, but the knowledge had to have been within her already to have allowed her to reach completion in hours rather than days.

Jarronn stretched and unsheathed his claws and gave a low purr before rising and shifting into his man's form. After he unlocked the door, he pushed it open and saw his fair Alice sprawled on the cushion on her belly, her blond tresses completely covering her face. Her hands were manacled just above her hips.

He eased up behind Alice and kissed first one ass

111

cheek, then the next. She moaned and arched her hips, and he smiled as he scented her immediate arousal. His cock responded by hardening to marble and it was only his tight control that kept him from entering her at once.

"Jarronn?" Alice murmured from beneath all that blond hair. She shifted her head but couldn't move the hair from her eyes with her wrists bound. "I—I mean Milord."

"Good morning, wench." With a twist of his fingers, her manacles vanished and he released her chain from the center ring.

Alice gave what could be a sigh or a moan as he helped her to a sitting position. Yes, something about her most definitely was different this morning, but she kept her head bowed and her tresses still hung in her face.

Using both his hands, he lifted the curtain of hair and pushed it away from her face. "You may look at me, Alice."

She raised her gaze to meet his and a tentative smile crossed her face. Her expression was lighter, less weighted, and satisfaction curled in his belly.

"Do you have something to say to me?" he asked. "You have permission to speak."

Alice sat up straighter and eyed him squarely. "I . . . I am beautiful, Milord."

Jarronn didn't allow his pleasure at her words to show in his expression. Instead he gave a slow nod. "Yes, Alice, you are very beautiful. It pleases me that you see yourself as you should."

Pink tinted her cheeks and she gave him a shy smile that slammed into his heart and soul like an anvil. If he didn't know better, he'd think this maiden had already won his heart. He produced a vial of orange blossom—scented *tili* oil and proceeded to rub it onto her wrists and arms. It would make any soreness or ache disappear at once. After sending the vial back to his chamber with his magic, Jarronn summoned a tiny bit of nourishing cake.

"This small amount will give you strength after being bound all night, but will do little for your hunger," he said as he held his palm out with the piece of white cake on it. "It is *eetmi* cake."

Alice giggled and then clapped her hand over her mouth and looked at him with her eyes wide. He raised an eyebrow and she dropped her hand to her lap and said, "I'm sorry, Milord. It just reminded me about this story about . . . never mind."

A few more small giggles escaped her as she ate the cake, but Jarronn simply watched her devour the treat.

When she had swallowed the last morsel, he helped her to her feet, then led her from the turret, through the castle, and toward the rainbow garden for their breakfast. In keeping with her training, he had her follow behind him, her head bowed and her hands behind her back.

The morning sunshine felt wonderful upon Alice's

skin as she followed Jarronn out of the castle and down the cool marble steps. It was amazing how much energy that one tiny piece of *eetmi* cake had given her. She bit her lip to stifle another giggle at the thought of that cake and how like Alice in Wonderland she truly was. Although this was a rather erotic wonderland.

And it was absolutely breathtaking.

She wondered at how the clouds were both green and blue and how clean and fresh everything smelled.

Alice also wondered at why she was in such a good mood after spending a night manacled and chained up. Maybe there was some kind of drug in that elixir and the cake that caused her outlook to be, well, perky.

The hearts swung at her nipples and her hair slid across her bare shoulders, and she almost stopped in her tracks as she realized there were other people outside the castle and in the garden that she and Jarronn were now walking through. Embarrassment flushed over her, but when she realized that most of them were naked, too, she decided what the hell.

Go with the flow, Alice.

Smells of roasted meat, baked breads, broiled vegetables, and sweet pastries met her nose as they reached a low table nestled in the gardens. When he stopped and turned toward her, Jarronn's stomach rumbled loud enough for her to hear, although it sounded more like a roar. The corner of Alice's mouth quirked and she glanced up at him from beneath her lashes. He returned her smile and instructed her to kneel at the table.

"Position," Jarronn reminded her, and Alice was

quick to put her hands behind her back and lower her eyes.

Almost dizzy with hunger, she eyed the display of unusual-looking dishes that right now smelled better than anything she'd ever smelled before. But why was Jarronn forcing her to kneel before the table? She thought about rebelling, just out of habit. Yet after last night . . . it was like she wasn't fighting this world anymore. Instead she was more accepting of it, as she was of herself.

Jarronn knelt beside her and from beneath her lashes she could see his erection.

He seemed to be waiting for her, so she asked, "May I eat now, Milord?"

"You may look at me," he said as he reached across the table and selected a morsel.

She kept her hands behind her back, and her mouth watered as he brought what looked like a heart-shaped cracker to her mouth. "Open," he commanded, and then slid the food into her mouth, his fingertips brushing over her lips and causing her to shiver.

Alice closed her eyes and moaned as the cracker thing melted on her tongue. It was similar to unleavened bread, topped with a creamy herbed paste, and it was incredible.

A hot, wet tongue swiped her nipple and she gasped as her eyes popped back open to see his dark head lowered and his tongue moving to her other breast. "Milord," she murmured, and arched up toward him, but he pulled away.

"Remember, my lovely Alice." The heart tattoo on his biceps rippled as he reached for another food item on the table, this one looking like a nickel-sized meatball. "You are here for my pleasure, not yours."

A shiver trailed her spine. *Wow.* What a charge that one simple statement gave her. He desired her for his pleasure. Somehow that made being with him even more exciting. This king could have anyone in his kingdom, the gorgeous Kalina even, yet he chose to be with Alice.

It reminded her again of their exchange of power— her submission for his pleasure.

Heady stuff.

"Open," he repeated, and slipped the little ball of food through her lips.

Immediately a burst of wild flavors erupted, nutty, spicy, and exotic. At the same moment Jarronn tweaked both her nipples hard enough that she would have cried out if her mouth weren't full.

The meal continued with Jarronn alternating by taking a bite of food for himself, then feeding Alice and erotically torturing her. She almost screamed when he made her eat a piece of red fruit that tasted like a mixture of pineapple, coconut, and honey while he slipped one finger between her thighs. The collar and chain and the crystal hearts dangling from her nipples were a constant reminder that she was his to command and control.

And she liked it. Liked it a lot.

With the way he was making her feel, so hot and wet

and needy, she wanted him to have his way with her and *now*.

When it came to dessert, Jarronn ordered her to rise up on her knees and thrust her breasts forward while widening her thighs. "Eat this sweetcake," he said as he slipped a heart-shaped piece of the golden substance into her mouth. While she chewed the dessert, he lowered down on his haunches like a tiger and drew his tongue along her soft folds. She almost came at once.

The sweetcake was heavy and chewy, locking her jaws together, and she couldn't speak to tell him she was close to climaxing. His light beard rubbed against her, stimulating her even further, and his eyes were on hers as he licked her again. Surely he could see what he was doing to her?

Her jaws still locked, Alice caught his gaze, asking him with her eyes if she could climax, but he shook his head, *no*.

She endured more strokes of his tongue and tried to fight off the orgasm, but it was far too powerful. A small shriek escaped her as the sweetcake dissolved and her jaws unlocked. While her hips rocked against his mouth, Jarronn pressed his face harder against her folds, lapping at her with his rough tongue and growling as he devoured her.

Fear curled in her belly, mixed with the intensity of her orgasm. She'd just come without his permission. Would he lock her up in the tower again?

Alice braced her hands against his shoulders to keep

herself from collapsing on him. "Jarronn—I mean Milord." She could barely speak, so intense were the sensations. "I can't take any more. I'm—I'm going to come again."

Jarronn raised himself up and Alice moved her hands off his shoulders and behind her back, and straightened the best she could do while feeling like she was going to melt into a puddle of goo.

He reached for her, grasped a handful of her hair, and dragged her roughly to him. All that kept her from falling forward was his hold on her. The pain of her hair being pulled was actually an enjoyable pain, one that made her ache for him to be even rougher with her. To take even more control of her.

"Tell me you're beautiful, Alice." His icy green gaze traveled down over her breasts, her waist, hips, and back to her face. "I want to hear it from your lips again."

"I . . ." She licked her lips. "I am beautiful, Milord."

"Again!" he demanded, releasing her.

Alice straightened, widening her knees, thrusting her breasts out, and raising her chin. "I *am* beautiful, Milord."

Jarronn gave her a feral smile. "Now for your punishment for reaching orgasm without my permission."

Oh, damn. She'd hoped he'd forgotten about that.

Although it depended on just how he intended to punish her.

He flicked his fingers at the table, plates, and leftovers, and everything vanished. Alice's jaw dropped and she cut her gaze from where the table had been and met Jarronn's eyes.

He held out his hand and her light blue hair ribbon appeared on his palm. Magic. Yup, the guy was magic. The real thing, not the Las Vegas act with white tigers and *what's he going to do with that?* she wondered as he approached her with the ribbon, then circled behind her. In a mere moment he tied the satin strip over her eyes, blindfolding her. It was wide, and thick enough that she couldn't see through the material.

"Such beautiful tresses," Jarronn murmured as he raked his fingers through her hair.

Since she could no longer see, the sensations were heightened and she shivered. But when his hand clasped the cold metal chain and slid down its length a feeling of fear and excitement rushed through her. He wouldn't hit her with the chain, would he? Not like Stone had whipped Jon with his chain. That was too much pain for her. No, she trusted Jarronn. He wouldn't do anything that would harm her.

She could almost relate to her ex, though—Jon with his nipple clamps, collar, and chain. The rings dangling from Alice's nipples kept them hard and constantly aroused, but she was real happy not to have clamps on them like Jon had.

The collar and chain . . . somehow that was power in itself. To know that she was responsible for Jarronn's pleasure was intoxicating.

"Come, wench," he growled in that deep sensual tone that made her grow wetter with anticipation, and he tugged on the chain.

Alice's legs almost refused to cooperate, she was so

nervous and excited. When she got to her feet, he pulled at the chain and she barely kept from stumbling forward.

"Do you trust me, Alice?" he asked as he led her across the grass. "If you do, then show it."

Despite the fact that she couldn't see where she was going, Alice straightened and kept her chin high, her hands clasped behind her back, forcing herself to walk without hesitation. "Yes, Milord. My trust is absolute."

A rumble rose up from Jarronn, sounding like the fierce jungle beast he had shifted from when Kalina first brought her from the castle. They walked for a while in silence, Alice imagining the stares of the king's subjects and finding the thought of people watching them surprisingly arousing. Eventually sounds, smells, and the very air changed, telling her they had left the rainbow gardens and entered the jungle.

Grass grew taller, reaching Alice's hips and brushing across her sensitized skin and her pussy as she blindly followed where he led her. Palm fronds skimmed her nipples and the hearts dangled in a wild dance against her breasts.

All around her the jungle sounds seemed louder, more intense. Scarier and more exciting. A waterfall thundered somewhere nearby, monkeys screeched, birds chattered and shrieked, and she couldn't help but shiver when she heard the cry of some kind of jungle cat, like a jaguar.

I trust Jarronn, she repeated in her thoughts, over and over, building confidence in the statement. *I trust him.*

Jarronn's cock had hardened until he was sure he

could use it for a spear. A fine weapon it would make, too.

A feeling of satisfaction surged through him as his future queen obediently followed him deeper into the jungle, trusting him. Already he sensed the changes in her becoming more complete. Indeed she was a fast learner, and born to rule at his side.

When he reached the sacred mating site, Jarronn stopped and was pleased when Alice responded immediately to the lessened pressure on the chain and stopped, too.

He wrapped the chain tight around his fist and tugged Alice hard enough to make her stumble toward him. She gasped when his erection brushed her belly and he sniffed the air, drinking in her intoxicating elixir. He brought his lips above hers and whispered, "Do you want your king to take you, wench?"

Alice visibly trembled, and when she licked her lips her tongue almost brushed his mouth. "Yes, Milord. I mean, if it would please you."

"Mayhap." Jarronn flicked the heart dangling from one nipple. "Or mayhap I would prefer to enjoy your mouth on my cock, wench."

"Whatever pleases you, Milord."

He smiled and wondered if she'd be so eager to please him as he said, "As punishment for reaching climax without permission, perhaps I should force you to watch me fuck one of my servants. Mayhap Kalina."

Dismay flashed across Alice's features and her mouth opened, then closed into a thin, tight line.

"I'm waiting," he murmured close to her ear.

"Would—would that please you, Milord?" she asked in a tone that said she would rather eat bark bees than watch him take another woman.

"It would please me to have my brothers join us." Jarronn paused and smiled at the look of shock and then curiosity that crossed her expression, and for a moment wished that she weren't blindfolded so that he might see her eyes. "Would you enjoy taking me and my brothers all at once, wench?"

"All four of you?" Alice's skin flushed and the scent of her desire was strong. "I . . . if it would please you, Milord."

With his magic, Jarronn retrieved the feathery leaf of a *ch'tok* tree. He let the fine chain slide between her breasts until the ring at the end settled at her mound. When he brushed the *ch'tok* leaf over her nipples, Alice gasped and arched toward his touch.

"*My* pleasure," he reminded her, and drew the feathery leaf down her belly and to her mons. "I will have Kalina shave you so that I might better see your delectable flesh." He knelt before her and pressed his hand to the inside of her thighs, and she automatically widened her stance. "Mmmm, yes. Such perfection."

Alice whimpered as he caressed the leaf over her. "Quiet, wench," he admonished her, and stroked the inside of her thighs. He leaned forward and ran his tongue along her soft skin. Her thighs trembled and he could tell it was taking effort for her to keep from moaning out loud.

He rose to his feet and slowly he circled her, enjoying the view of her gently curved body, her full, perfect breasts, and her well-rounded hips. When he stood behind her, he lifted her long hair and pushed it over one of her shoulders so that it was out of his way. By the skies, his cock would surely burst if he did not take her soon.

Alice shivered and it was all she could do to hold back another moan. This man was torturing her, driving her out of her mind. More so than before, if that was possible. She wanted him inside her so badly she could scream.

His pleasure. She was supposed to be thinking about his, not hers. If she truly trusted him, she had to believe he would give her what she needed. Well, he was certainly receiving great pleasure from teasing her, drawing out her arousal and his own.

She wasn't sure if she could take much more of his pleasure. It was about to drive her nuts.

Jarronn continued his sensual assault, trailing something light and feathery, yet different, over her skin. Without her sight, all her other senses were heightened. She could smell the rich loam of the jungle, the fragrant perfume of orchids, and countless other scents she couldn't identify.

Biting her lower lip, Alice held back another moan as Jarronn skimmed the feathery thing over each of her ass cheeks and between, then the back of each thigh. He took his time, moving down to the backs of her knees, to her ankles, and then worked his way back up.

123

If it weren't for the fact that she knew he'd add another punishment, she would have screamed.

Finally, Jarronn rose up behind Alice and pressed his hard, muscular body against her softer, rounder form. Her heart pounded so loudly it nearly drowned out the jungle sounds of animals and the roar of the waterfall. He thrust his erection against her clasped hands and she moved her fingers around his length as he slid back and forth.

"How shall I punish you, sweet wench?" he murmured beside her ear, and she quivered at the thought of what he might come up with. "I believe I would find it most pleasurable to spank you."

CHAPTER EIGHT

A LICE'S BREATHING HITCHED AS JARRONN grabbed her chain and led her forward several steps. Even though she was still blindfolded, she forced herself to walk with confidence, proving her trust in him.

After he told her to stop, he drew her hands from behind her back and brought them in front of her. "Do not move your feet." He guided her by taking her hands in his, pulling her forward, and forcing her to bend until he placed her palms against a flat, uneven surface that reached her waist level. "Widen your thighs, wench."

God but she loved it when he called her wench in that sexy purr of his.

As she spread her legs, balmy jungle air caressed her ass. Her breasts felt large and weighted, as if the crystal hearts were pulling them down toward the ground.

Jarronn moved behind her and rubbed his callused hand over her ass. "Why are you being punished?"

"For climaxing without permission, Milord." Alice tensed, waiting for that first slap, and her insides tingled. Good grief, she was going to be spanked. She'd never even been spanked as a child, much less an adult. But what was really strange was how badly she wanted Jarronn to spank her.

"As you know, disobedience will not be tolerated." Jarronn moved his mouth down her back to her hips, then rubbed his soft beard over her ass in a smooth and sensual movement. He kissed each of her butt cheeks, flicking his tongue against the flesh, and she moaned.

"Quiet, wench," he ordered in a deep and commanding tone. "You may not speak or make a sound. Nod if you understand."

She nodded, causing her hair to slide across her face and the satin blindfold. When his fingers moved from her ass cheeks and into her folds, she trembled. She lowered her forehead against the flat, rocky surface in front of her and focused on holding in her sounds of ecstasy. She would *not* disappoint him.

When had it become so important to her to please Jarronn?

Alice managed to contain her moans at the feel of him stroking her, but her thighs quivered and she could barely keep from squirming. He eased his fingers from her. As she shuddered with excitement, her chain clinked against the rock's surface.

"Such a splendid ass," he murmured, and gently pushed his finger into her tight anus. She all but choked to keep down her gasp from the incredible sensation.

Somehow Jarronn's finger sliding into her was better than any dildo or butt plug she'd used before.

"To be sure, you would enjoy my cock here, would you not, wench?" He slid a second finger inside and pumped both in and out of her anus. In the next second a large hand swatted her across one ass cheek with a resounding slap.

A cry rose up in Alice's throat that she barely contained. His swat stung yet made her even more excited, and wetter than ever. She braced her legs and raised her ass toward him as he thrust his finger in and out and continued to spank her, swat after swat. The sound of his hand slapping her ass rang through the air again and again. It stung; it felt good. It hurt; it made her horny beyond belief. It was more than pleasure, more than pain . . . it was *indescribable*.

While he spanked and finger-fucked her, she gradually slipped into a state of euphoria where her mind reveled in the sensations. Here she found she could give up control of her orgasm to Jarronn and she no longer had to fight to keep back her moans and sounds of pleasure. She would make him pleased with her. He had already shown her more caring and consideration than any man in her life had done.

The spanking stopped and he withdrew his fingers from her anus, making her feel empty. He murmured soft words of praise as he kissed the stinging flesh of her ass. "Such a good wench," he said as he laved his tongue across her hot skin. "You are perfect."

Gently he eased his arm around Alice's waist and

caught her to him. "You are lovelier than I had dared to dream," he murmured.

Alice's body was so stimulated, so aroused, yet she managed to stay in that state where it felt like her body was not her own . . . she was Jarronn's to do with as he wished.

While he pressed his muscled body tight against her softer form, he kissed the back of her neck, his beard teasing the delicate skin. With deft fingers he pulled at the ends of the ribbon blindfolding her, and the satin fell away.

The sudden light caused Alice to blink, even though she was apparently in a darker part of the jungle. On one level she was cognizant of the new surroundings, while on another she was completely aware of everything that Jarronn was doing to her. The way his hands felt upon her breasts, his lips caressing her nape and his cock pressed against the cleft in her ass.

She tilted her head back, leaning into him, and saw the feathery blue leaves of a tree like the one she'd first woken beneath when she'd tumbled into this wonderland. Surrounding them were wide-leaved jungle plants and vines and countless sweet-perfumed orchids in pastel shades of pinks, purples, yellows, and blues.

Before she had a chance to realize what he was doing, Jarronn turned her around to face him so fast she almost cried out in surprise. In an effortless movement, he grabbed her by the waist and placed her still-stinging ass on the rock she'd just braced herself against. His features took on a feral, hungry look as he used the satin ribbon blindfold to tie her wrists together. She watched with a combination of fear and fascination as he produced a red silk scarf, then raised her arms and fastened her wrists to a branch overhead.

Jarronn pushed his hands against her knees, widening her thighs so that she was completely exposed. With her arms fastened overhead, her breasts jutting forward, and her legs spread wide, she felt even more excited and wanton than ever.

"You have permission to speak." Jarronn's ice-green eyes were filled with a wild lust that made her shiver with anticipation. "Tell me, what would you like, wench?"

Alice flicked her tongue against her lower lip. A thousand ideas occurred to her, but she still drifted in that almost place, that space of relaxation and surrender—and suddenly she knew the right answer. "I wish for your pleasure, Milord."

"My pleasure now is to fuck you." He grasped his cock and moved his hand up and down its impressive length. "You will watch me take you, Alice. And when you see my cock buried in you, you will have no doubt that you belong to me."

You belong to me, his words echoed in her thoughts, welcoming her. She belonged to this fine king who was sexier and more powerful than any man she'd ever known.

Alice swallowed. Great sex and a Dom who thought she was beautiful . . . She could live with that.

Jarronn pressed the head of his cock to her wet core. "Tell me."

"I belong to you, Milord," she whispered.

"Watch," he commanded, and she obeyed, her gaze dropping to where his cock waited at her entrance.

With a feral roar, Jarronn thrust himself into her.

Alice cried out, pulling against the bonds that fastened her to the tree. The feel of him inside her was amazing. His cock filled her, stretched her, completed her.

She was dying of pleasure as she watched him moving in and out of her core. She'd never seen anything so incredible in all her life as the sight of Jarronn fucking her. Her scent and his surrounded them.

Abruptly he stopped and Alice whimpered.

"I want you wild for me," Jarronn ordered at the same time an intense, vibrant musk emanated from him. "Beg me to fuck you."

Alice started trembling. Sweat coated her skin and every atom of her body burst into awareness.

"Fuck me, Milord." She fought her bindings and thrashed against Jarronn. "Please fuck me!"

He clenched her hips with his hands and drove in and out of her. Harder and faster until everything blurred around her. Sights, smells, sounds of the jungle and their frantic sex whirled together.

A powerful orgasm built up in her, and she knew it would be nuclear when it was unleashed. "Please let me come, Milord," she begged.

"I want to hear your cries." He let out a growl and she saw the untamed beast in his gaze. "You may come for me *now*."

Alice belted out a scream that she was sure would reach the ears of every person in the whole damn country. The atomic blast of her climax expanded, growing larger and larger, spreading through every fraction of her body, and leaving nothing in its path untouched. She couldn't stop screaming, couldn't stop pumping her hips against his and begging for more.

Orgasm after orgasm ripped through her, and when she was sure she couldn't take another one Jarronn gave a roar and came, releasing his hot fluid into her core. He continued to pump in and out of her, spurring her spasms until he finally stopped and drew her close.

The musk vanished and the wildness within Alice settled, dissipating almost as quickly as it had come on. It left her so limp that if she weren't tied to the tree branch, she would have collapsed onto the boulder into a well-pleasured, exhausted, and damn near comatose heap.

Jarronn nuzzled her neck and nipped at her earlobe. "Beautiful. You are so beautiful, Alice." The way he spoke to her and touched her made her feel like she was his queen.

Oh, my god. I just fucked a king!

They were still joined together, his cock still amazingly hard inside her. His sweat-coated muscles flexed as he raised his hands to the scarf and ribbon binding her wrists and released her.

After rubbing her wrists, Jarronn drew her into his embrace. Alice sighed and wrapped her arms around his waist, pressing her breasts against his solid chest, their sweat mingling and the smells of their sex a satisfying reminder of the most mind-blowing experience she could ever hope to have in her lifetime.

A feeling of complete and total happiness nearly overwhelmed her with its intensity. She wanted this moment to last forever. Right after he fucked her senseless again.

Jarronn kissed the damp hair at her forehead and murmured, "You are mine, Alice O'Brien. You belong to me."

In her sleep Alice rubbed the tip of her nose against Jarronn's chest, and he smiled. They were reclined upon a blanket beneath the *ch'tok* tree where he had taken her for the first time . . . and several more times after that. He had fucked her mouth, her quim, and her lovely tight anus.

With a mind-command he had summoned a meal for him and his sexually insatiable woman, and after they had eaten, Alice had fallen asleep.

Yes, her training was coming along more quickly and more perfectly than he had dared to hope. Soon, very soon, she would be ready to mind-bond with his brothers, mayhap within a week or so.

If she wasn't fully ready and the bonding was attempted, then it could prove disastrous. On the other hand, if they waited too long, Mikaela or her *bakirs* might penetrate Alice's consciousness with their infernal mind-spells when she wasn't with Jarronn. He feared Alice's innate psychic strength would not be enough to protect her. But until her training was complete, he would keep her in her quarters and spell the room against invasion.

Wind rustled through the *ch'tok* tree's leaves and afternoon sunlight sparkled through them and played upon Alice's features. Her eyelids fluttered and then she gave him a sleepy smile. "Hi . . . Milord."

Jarronn pressed his lips to her forehead and inhaled her scent that had long ago imprinted itself upon every molecule in his body. He would be able to find her, no matter where she might be within his kingdom, just by following her scent-trail. "Did you sleep well?"

"Yes, Milord." She pursed her lips as though in thought and seemed to come to a decision. "May I ask you some questions?"

He raised an eyebrow and pushed himself up so that he was braced on one elbow looking down at her. "That would depend. What is it you wish to know?"

"About you, Milord." Alice dropped her gaze and studied her hands. "I want to know more about you. What you were like as a child. What kind of mischief you got into with your brothers, how you shape-shift into a tiger. And other things."

Jarronn studied Alice's features as he considered her request. He rose to his feet and held out his hand to her. "Come."

While he helped her to stand he couldn't help but admire her lovely curves and the way her large breasts bounced as she moved. When she stood before him, she automatically assumed the position of respect and bowed her head. He smoothed his fingers over her blond hair that was mussed about her face and tangled from their lovemaking.

"Look at me, Alice."

When she raised her eyes to meet his, he smiled. "For this moment in time, you may ask me any questions you wish to, and we will speak as equals."

Alice's smile lit up her expression. "Thank you."

"What would you like to know first?" Jarronn asked as he led her along a well-worn path.

"Why must I always stand in the position of respect?" She tilted her head to look up at him as they skirted a burred palm. "Sometimes it pisses me off."

It pleased him that her spunk remained despite her apparent acceptance of her role. As queen she would not need to remain submissive in public—only respectful and always showing her absolute loyalty. However, by Tarok law she must first complete her training and demonstrate unquestioning trust and faith in him before he could inform her of her future position. In addition, she would also need to go through the mind-bonding with him and his brothers.

He settled for what he thought would be enough for her to know for the time being.

"It is important that you always show your subservience to me before my subjects." Jarronn pushed aside a flowered-vine curtain and held it up for Alice to walk under. "I am High King of Tarok, and amongst my people such respect is expected. If one person does not show respect, loyalty, and trust, it could cause others to believe there is a flaw in my leadership."

Alice looked thoughtful and nodded. "I see. What about when we're alone? Can there be Jarronn and Alice time, rather than just Milord and wench?"

The corner of his mouth quirked. "For you, Alice, I will do this. But only at rare times when we are alone, and only if you behave in public."

She gave him a teasing grin. "And if I'm bad, you'll spank me, right?"

Jarronn swatted her ass and she yelped. "Yes, wench."

He continued to hold her hand as they walked through the jungle and he answered each of her questions, pleased that she wanted to know more about him as he wanted to learn all that he could about her. When she asked how old he was, Alice stumbled, her apparent shock so great when he told her that he was over 240 Earth years old.

She stared at him in amazement. "But you look like you're in your late thirties at the most."

Jarronn shrugged. "Everyone ages differently in my world."

A furrow formed between her brows. "Do you even remember being a child?" He laughed and this time her expression was one of surprise. "I've never heard you laugh before."

"Odder happenings have occurred." He squeezed her hand as they continued their walk through the jungle he had grown up in. "I remember everything that has happened in my lifetime."

She tilted her head up as she looked at him. "Doesn't your brain get too full of stuff?"

He led her through a maze of hanging travel-vines. "Everything is simply stored until it is needed."

"Well, that's cool." Alice ducked around the vines and tossed her hair over her shoulder. "Please tell me some of the things you did as a child."

Talking with Alice brought back fond memories of his youth, and she laughed out loud when he shared with her the more humorous instances. She giggled when he told her about the time he and Darronn had used magic adhesive to glue all the cooking spoons and pots to the kitchen tables and were punished by being forced to prepare a meal for every one of the almost one hundred residents of the castle, including servants.

He also told her about a more serious instance when he, Darronn, Karn, and Ty snuck out of the castle in the middle of the night as tigers when they were just cubs. They stumbled across the path of a full-grown jaguar and barely escaped with their lives. As they had run from the jaguar, the beast raked its claws over Karn's chest, and he still bore the scars. Being the eldest, Jarronn had always felt responsible for Karn's injury, and from that point forward he did all he could to protect those he loved.

"How is it you can shape-shift into a white tiger?" Alice brushed an orchid out of her face as they ducked beneath a low-hanging branch full of the blooms. "Can everyone here do it?"

"Not everyone . . . no." How to explain generations of crossbreeding in a mere fraction of time? "We are weretigers, but unfortunately few of us remain." He clenched his teeth and then forced the words out: "For almost twenty Tarok years, no weretiger cub has been born." He didn't endeavor to explain why . . . that would come later.

"Weretiger." Alice shivered but didn't look dismayed or frightened. "Everything here is just so different and so overwhelming."

When she asked about his parents, he explained how they had divided the kingdom into four parts before their deaths. They had passed on to the golden lands just over two Tarok decades ago.

While they continued walking through the jungle, to his surprise Jarronn even expressed a bit of his concern for Darronn. He had always pushed himself to succeed, always competing against Jarronn, who was but hours older and had inherited all that came with being a first-born son.

"You're a twin, too?" Alice glanced up at him, her eyes wide. "Alexi is a couple of minutes older than me. I guess in some ways I've been competitive against her."

Jarronn gripped Alice's hand as he helped her step over a large fallen tree. "Are you angry with her for being who she is?"

"No." Alice shook her head as she made it over the log and then frowned. "Well, I guess I have been, in the past . . . a lot. I love my sister, but she's always had the greatest share of attention. All I heard growing up was that Alexi is so beautiful and that I should diet until I'm as thin as Alexi, that I should have made better grades like Alexi, or that I should have been a lawyer like Alexi, instead of a secretary." She shrugged and looked up at Jarronn. "Yeah, I love her, but sometimes it downright sucked being her sister."

"How do you feel now?" Jarronn asked softly.

"Honestly . . ." Her expression was one of seriousness yet happiness and confusion all at once. "At this moment I wouldn't change who I am for anything in your world or mine."

A surge of triumph rose up within Jarronn. He stopped beneath a large cluster of orchids and pressed Alice up against the glossy trunk of a *ch'tok* tree. She gasped as she looked up into his eyes and she surely read the hunger and need in his gaze.

He grasped her waist and settled his hands at her hips. "Hold on to me."

She slipped her arms around his neck, her lips parted, expectant and waiting.

Jarronn's mouth met Alice's in a possessive yet gentle kiss. Without words he told her what his heart was already saying. No matter that he had known her but days, his soul had known her forever. He loved her so deeply . . . that it in itself was pain mixed with pleasure. A fierce ache in his heart that could only be fulfilled by Alice.

He wouldn't tell her of his love until after her training, when he was ready to make her his queen.

A purr rose up within his chest as he thrust his tongue into Alice's mouth. The scent of their sex mingled was one of the most intoxicating smells he'd ever experienced.

She clung to him as their mouths devoured each other, feeding their needs in ways that only two soul mates could fulfill.

Jarronn grabbed her thighs and raised them up, and she wrapped her legs around his hips. Without breaking the kiss, he guided his cock into her waiting core and thrust home into her slick heat.

With slow, deliberate thrusts, Jarronn fucked Alice, taking his pleasure from her body while giving her all that he could. She moaned inside his mouth, and the sound made his cock even harder. He forced himself to keep the pace slow, drawing out this moment for as long as he possibly could.

Alice tore her mouth from his, her eyes wild and her body shaking. "May I come, Milord?"

"Yes." He thrust harder now. "Give me your orgasm, Alice. Come for me."

When she started to cry out with her release, Jarronn locked his mouth to hers, drawing her sounds of completion into his soul. Her core contracted around his cock in pulse after pulse after pulse. By the skies he wanted to remain like this, his cock deep inside her and taking her over and over again.

His own climax tore through him and he threw his head back and roared.

When Jarronn escorted her back to the castle, a little of Alice's euphoria waned once he told her that he was leaving her alone for the night. He brought her to the room where she had woken the very first day she landed in his kingdom—where he had bound her to the bed with silk scarves.

"I have business to attend to." Jarronn grabbed the chain on her collar and pulled her to him when her expression gave away her disappointment. "Dinner will be served in your quarters, and a servant shall attend to your needs. I will come for you again on the morrow, wench."

He gave her a fierce kiss that caused her to moan with need for him. As many times as he'd used her body for their mutual pleasure today and as sore as she was from head to toe, how could she want him now?

"Remember the rules." He released her and strode toward the open doorway. Resting one hand on the door frame, he looked back to her. "As always, remember your promise to me, my beautiful Alice."

She gasped as he shape-shifted into a gorgeous white tiger—or *weretiger*. It was simply breathtaking to watch his features change, his body elongate, and all that glorious white-and-black-striped fur cover his skin. In the same motion that brought his front paws to the floor he turned and bounded into the darkened hallway.

Good lord. I just spent the day fucking a weretiger.

It felt as though a part of her left with him, yet at the same time she felt a little relieved at having time away from his intense presence. She hadn't even been able to go to the bathroom without him nearby, and she'd had to go in the jungle for cripes sake. He'd said something about losing all her inhibitions and understanding that what came naturally to her body should never embarrass her.

Yeah, well, she'd still like to pee in peace. Although she hadn't said it to him exactly like that.

While Jarronn had walked her back to the castle, Alice had felt like she was skipping across the Tarok blue-green clouds. She'd never felt so sated, so *loved*, in all her life. Yes, her sister, aunt, cousin, and friends loved her, but this was *different*.

Although love . . . that was a word she hadn't intended to use with any man again. Not after Steve and Jon, the assholes.

But Jarronn . . . he was incredible. He was a *real* man. Powerful and dominant, yet strong and wise, caring and loving.

Alice sighed and moved her hand to her collar and smiled. Okay, so he could be an ass sometimes, too, but all in all he was pretty damn incredible.

CHAPTER NINE

A T LEAST A WEEK WENT BY, ACCORDING TO Tarok days, and Alice was spending another lonely night in her quarters, where Jarronn left her every evening. Scented candles flickered upon every surface save the bed, and tonight the room smelled of jasmine incense and plum spice. She'd just had her dinner and a bath, and her skin felt clean and tingly and alive.

If only Jarronn hadn't left her alone again.

Even though the days passed too quickly for her, here there were approximately thirty-nine Earth hours in a single Tarok day, so she'd actually been gone over two Earth weeks. Most of her time was spent with Jarronn, but her nights were always by herself. He said it was necessary to her training and that if she continued to progress so quickly she'd be able to join him in his bed soon. Just the thought of sleeping in his strong arms each night and waking up beside him was enough to make her shiver with excitement.

With Jarronn present, Kalina had shaved Alice's mound so that the skin was soft and smooth. The king rather enjoyed licking her, and having it bare made the sensations all the more intense.

She sighed as she moved to the open window of her room and stared out into the night. The air was still and not even a breeze stirred. From her room she had a breathtaking view of the Kingdom of Hearts, and she especially liked to see it at night. Warm light glowed in cottage windows and she caught the light smell of wood smoke from the hearth fires. Mingling with the smoke were the sweet scents of the zillions of flowers growing in Jarronn's rainbow gardens.

Alice's nipples ached as she thought about how she and Jarronn had fucked just about everywhere remotely private around this castle, including the rainbow garden. She couldn't get enough of him.

Her days . . . *omigod,* they were incredible. She'd become so used to being Jarronn's sub that his rules came automatically to her and she no longer felt shame or embarrassment when she was naked in front of other people. Hell, most of the time everyone else was naked, too. In Tarok people were all sizes, shapes, and hues of the rainbow, just like Earth, except here everyone was appreciated for who they were.

After just over one week with Jarronn, Alice was sure she was a born submissive . . . well, born to be *his* sub. It was the most amazing feeling—to give up control of her needs, her fears, her inhibitions, and to just be herself.

She also enjoyed their "Jarronn and Alice" time, when it was just the two of them and they talked and interacted as equals. It seemed odd to admit to herself, though, that she craved his dominance more than she needed to be on equal footing with him. Or maybe it was how much she enjoyed having power over his pleasure, and the incredible high it gave her to please him.

And yes, she knew she was beautiful. She felt comfortable with the admission and the sense of freedom that came with it.

Alice couldn't get over how accustomed to the collar she'd become and how much she enjoyed the caress of the fine silver chain as it swung back and forth across her naked hips whenever she moved. It was a symbol of ownership, and Jarronn owned her. Not like a slave but as a treasured possession, and she really liked how it felt to belong to him.

A sly grin curved the corner of her mouth. On occasion she deliberately disobeyed him, just so that he'd spank her or use his red flogger. She never did anything that would cause him to award her a more severe punishment. *Cripes,* she certainly didn't want to end up in that damn turret again. But sometimes she'd climax without permission or she'd let a moan slip out when he told her not to. She had the feeling that he rather enjoyed dealing out those lesser punishments as much as she enjoyed receiving them.

She smiled at the beauty of her own private kingdom view. It was far different from what she'd grown up with in San Francisco. No streetlights, cars, or stoplights. No sirens, no trolley clanging and clattering along the tracks, no roar of traffic.

But of course all the things she loved about the City by the Bay were not here, either . . . walking along Ocean Beach on a Saturday morning with the thick fog rolling out, the view of the Golden Gate Bridge and Alcatraz from the Pier, the tremendous diversity of people and cultures.

And if she stayed here in this wonderland she'd never see her sister again, not to mention her cousin Annie, her aunt Awai, or her best friend, Maryam. What were they all thinking? That maybe she'd been murdered and tossed into the San Francisco Bay? Alice hated the thought of them being worried over her and she wished she could have her small circle of family and friends with her here.

An ache blossomed in her chest and she bit back the sudden urge to cry. For the first time since arriving in this beautiful but bizarre world, Alice felt a true sense of homesickness settle in her belly.

At the same time she was torn by her enjoyment of this land and what she'd experienced so far. Even though she hadn't been here very long, she felt like she had been here for months.

Alice also had to admit that she certainly didn't miss a culture that dismissed its heavier citizens. A culture that ridiculed people of size and constantly forced weight-loss advertisements on them. Of course all the ads had perfect-bodied mannequins who made a gal with a few extra pounds want to go out and eat a whole damn cheesecake just for spite.

Yeah, Tarok could certainly be a much better place to live. If only she had all the people she loved here to share it with.

Turning her back on her view, Alice went around the room and snuffed out the candles save the one beside her bed. After she crawled beneath the soft quilted cover, she blew out the candle and lay on her back. For a while she stared at the ceiling, thinking about her friends and her small family but mostly about Alexi. How was she doing? She'd always been overprotective, and now she must be thinking that Alice had been kidnapped or murdered.

A hot tear rolled down her cheek and she brushed it away with the back of her hand and snuffled. If only there was a way to bring Alexi here, everything would be perfect.

And if this was truly a perfect world, maybe Jarronn would even fall in love with Alice.

A cold and harsh wind swept through the window and Alice shivered beneath her cover.

"Wake up, Alice dear!" a woman cooed in a singsong baby voice. "You are such a lazy and fat girl that you would just sleep the day away if I allowed you to."

Confusion swirled through Alice as she slowly eased up in bed and stared at the slender woman standing by the window, the sheer curtains flapping behind her in the chill wind. Golden moonlight and the glow of candles illuminated the woman's features. She had long wheat-blond hair and she wore a tight black leather catsuit with a neckline that dropped in a V from her breasts down to her exposed belly button. The V was so wide that Alice could see the full curves of the woman's breasts almost to her nipples and down to the peculiar tattoo around her navel that looked like a large cat's paw print.

The woman snapped a leather whip and snarled. With a gasp, Alice recoiled and her stomach clenched. She had no doubt this woman was a Dominatrix and if given the chance she would flay Alice until her skin was bloody.

"Fat bitch." The Domme curled her lip and lashed the whip again. It was so long that Alice felt the movement of it through the air and the sting of leather against her cheek.

Alice cried out and brought her hand to her face and cradled it, as if that might protect her from the Domme. "What are you doing in my room?"

"How could you ever think the king could love the likes of you?" The woman tossed her head and gave a wicked smile. "You're fat and ugly and no one will ever love you."

Lower lip trembling, Alice shook her head. "You're wrong. I'm b-beautiful. And Jarronn does care for me."

"Sure he cares for you . . . for a fuck or a few." The Domme made a tsking sound and shook her head. "Alice, Alice. When will you learn that you're just not good enough?"

Tears started rolling down Alice's face and she could barely speak. "I—I'm not ugly."

"Why do you think Steve and Jon fucked around on you? Jarronn, too, will soon find a woman more to his liking. Perhaps he already has, these many long nights away from you."

The Domme grinned, her expression triumphant. "You're noth-ing, Alice. A big, fat nothing."

"No!" Alice bolted upright in bed, her cheeks wet with tears, and she blinked at the sheer curtains lying completely motionless to either side of the window. She was still in her castle quarters and it was nighttime, but her candles were unlit and there wasn't a whip-wielding Dominatrix standing in front of her window.

A sob burst from Alice. She wrapped her arms tight around her knees, buried her face against them, and cried.

It had only been a nightmare, but it had seemed so incredibly real. A lifetime of pain and hurts assaulted her, as though the woman from the dream had caused every last one to be unleashed.

No doubt Jarronn would marry someone slender and gorgeous who would be his queen. Alice would be sent away as his former submissive, or maybe he'd make her his servant, forcing her to do chores while he was with his queen.

An overwhelming feeling of despair filled Alice, weighting her entire body with shame, and she cried even harder. How could she have so easily believed that Jarronn could come to love her? There was nothing beautiful or special about her at all.

A powerful sense that something was wrong burst through Jarronn and jolted him from his sleep. He shifted into a tiger and loped through the castle to Alice's quarters. Even before he got there, he sensed his warding had been breached. He bounded into the room and his gut clenched when he saw Alice huddled on her bed and heard her sobs.

Effortlessly Jarronn shifted into his human form. After lighting the room's candles, he eased onto the bed beside his future queen and drew her into his arms. She startled, then allowed herself to relax against him.

"A nightmare?" He posed it as a question, but he knew the answer before she nodded. Her silken hair slid across his chest with the movement of her head. "I can't hear you, Alice."

"Y-yes, Milord." She sniffed and tried to pull away. "I had a nightmare, but I . . . I'm fine."

Every fiber of his being told him that she was lying and that she was not all right at all. "Explain to me what your dream was about."

Alice sniffed. "I don't want to talk about it, Milord."

"You know better than to disobey my orders." He brushed her hair from her face and tilted her head back, forcing her to look up at him. "Tell me every last detail of this dream."

"Yes, Milord." Her tears wet his chest and her voice trembled as she told him about the Dominatrix in her dream and what the woman had said.

Mikaela. The bitch had indeed broken through all his protections and had used Alice's insecurities to attack her. One night's mindspell should not do any permanent harm, but he would have to move quickly and forcefully to undo the damage Mikaela had done.

"Alice, you have broken your promise to me." Jarronn kept his voice firm and his gaze steady as he studied her tear-drenched face. "You promised to love yourself, and that includes not allowing anything or anyone to cause you to feel otherwise."

"But—but, Milord." Alice shook her head, and from her expression he could tell she knew exactly what punishment he intended for her. "It was a nightmare. Only a dream. Why would you punish me for that?"

"Are you questioning me?" He eased away from Alice and off of her bed as he spoke and made his tone even harder. "Is further punishment required?"

She dropped her gaze to the bed. "No, Milord."

"Out of bed." Jarronn stepped back and watched as Alice tried to hold back her sniffles while she avoided his eyes. She climbed off the bed and stood in the position of respect.

"Follow me," he commanded, and did not look back to see if she followed. He had no doubt that she would, just as there was no question in his mind that he must act quickly. It could mean the difference between Alice's life and death if she was not properly trained before the bonding.

And it was more urgent than ever that the bonding take place as soon as possible.

When Alice woke again, she was in the turret room, manacled and chained to the middle of the floor and lying on her side on the big red cushion. Sunlight streaming through the window was bright, telling her that it had to be well into the morning. She felt amazingly clearheaded and serene.

At first she'd been hurt that Jarronn had chained her up again last night, but after he gave her more of that *Drink Me* potion she'd calmed down and mentally worked through the lesson he was endeavoring to teach her.

It didn't matter if it was a dream or if it had been an attack by a real person, Alice must have unwavering strength of belief in herself. And regardless, she must believe in Jarronn. Her trust in him and his words and opinions had to be absolute.

The nightmare persistently hung in the background of her mind, and it was odd how clearly she remembered it. However, she was now able to analyze it. Last night she had treated it like a movie, playing the dream backward and forward in her mind, slow, then fast, with the volume shut completely off, until she wanted to giggle at the image of the Dominatrix silently yapping like one of those old movies.

The more she worked the dream over in her mind, the more Alice realized everything in that dream came down to the power of words. If she didn't allow them to have power over her, then that's all they were . . . words. Nothing more, nothing less.

Amazing how much clearer it all was now, and how simple it really was. *Sticks and stones . . .*

The heavy clump of boots sounded outside the turret door, and excitement at seeing Jarronn filled her. As the key turned in the lock Alice struggled to a kneeling position, which wasn't easy considering her hands were bound. By the time the door was opened, she was on her knees and facing it, her head bowed, ready for him.

But as she glanced from beneath her lashes, she realized the man standing before her wasn't Jarronn.

Slowly she raised her gaze from the man's black boots to his black pants, over his naked, muscular chest, only to meet the fierce scowl of Darronn, her king's twin. His arms were folded and he studied her as though trying to determine her worth.

Fluttering erupted in her belly, but she simply tilted her chin and eyed him back. He wasn't her Dom and she didn't have to drop her gaze in his presence. What the hell was he doing here, anyway?

A gold hoop earring glinted at Darronn's left ear as he gave an abrupt nod like coming to some internal decision. "You are ready for the bonding." He made a gesture with his hand. Her manacles vanished and her chain was unhooked from the ring in the floor.

She found herself holding her breath as she rose to her feet and forced herself to breathe. But when Darronn strode across the room to stand but inches from her, Alice thought seriously about running. The man was fierce and intense, and anger seemed to radiate below his surface. With his attitude, the gold earring, and the spade tattoo at his wrist he reminded her of a real bad boy—all he needed was a leather jacket and a Harley.

When Darronn reached her, he held out his palm and a much larger piece of *eetmi* cake appeared than what Jarronn had given her. But this time Alice didn't feel inclined to laugh as she accepted the cake.

"Your breakfast. You will need strength for the bonding." He casually twisted one of her heart nipple rings, tweaking the tender nub and causing Alice to gasp. He released it as he said, "Yes . . . you are a lovely wench."

Alice stepped back, but already he had turned and was headed toward the door. He paused and cast a glance over his shoulder. "Come, wench. *Now.*"

She didn't budge. Who was he to order her around? "Not until you tell me where Jarronn is and where you're taking me."

Darronn's scowl deepened and the muscles in his naked chest flexed with raw power. "My brother awaits my return with you. Follow or I shall toss your lovely ass over my shoulder and carry you."

Okeydokey.

With a gulp and even more butterflies in her belly, Alice started forward and followed the imposing man out of the turret room and down the steps. Jarronn's twin was dark and mysterious, and scary as hell. She was sure glad that Darronn hadn't been the one to find her and make her his sub. Heaven help any woman who had to give up control to him.

It occurred to her that she was still carrying the *eetmi* cake, only she'd squished it a bit in her hand when Darronn twisted her nipple ring. The piece of cake was absolutely huge. What exactly was this bonding he was talking about that she'd need so much strength for? Jarronn had mentioned something about her going through a bonding, but he'd never explained.

Feeling more than a little off balance, Alice nibbled at the piece of white cake as she followed Darronn through the castle. A sense of dismay flooded over her when he took her into a different turret at the southeast corner of the castle. Was she going to be locked up yet again?

By the time they walked up step after step and reached the top of the turret, Alice had finished the cake and she had so much energy she figured she'd be bouncing off the walls once they made it into the turret room. She wasn't the least bit out of breath. If anything, she was raring to go.

When Darronn held open the door and ushered her in, everything seemed to skid to a halt. She was in a beautiful round red velvet room—but good lord, what were all the contraptions filling the place? Leather and chains and wooden crosses, a swing-looking thing, and a golden ring suspended in midair.

Rich mahogany divans, chairs, and settees, all covered in red velvet cushions, were scattered around the plush carpeted room. But what made her heart beat so fast that she thought it would burst from her chest and fly out the room's single window was the sight of the three naked kings reclining on all that red-velvet furniture. The door slammed behind her and the lock's click was loud in the silence. Darronn walked around her to the middle of the room, made a simple gesture with his hand, and all his clothes vanished, too.

Oh. My. God.

She could only stare at the four most perfect *naked* male bodies she'd ever seen. And the four kings were all looking at Alice as if they were going to devour her.

CHAPTER TEN

"Come here, Alice." Jarronn's deep voice cut through the silence and Alice's shock.

Automatically responding to his command, she refused to look at the other kings and walked to the divan where Jarronn reclined. Her feet sank into the plush red carpeting and her whole body quivered with apprehension and excitement.

When she reached his side, he shook his head. "Alice, you disappoint me."

Heat rushed through her as she realized that she'd been shocked into forgetting to stand in the position of respect the moment she was in his presence. She bowed her head, clasped her hands behind her back, and widened her stance.

"You do realize that I must punish you now?" Jarronn asked.

Her scalp tingled and she was certain this was not

going to be an ordinary punishment. "Yes, Milord," she murmured.

"Darronn." Her king gestured within her line of sight, the heart tattoo flexing on his biceps. Her heart beat faster as she heard the soft fall of footsteps upon the carpet and then Darronn stood beside her.

"Kneel before my brother, Alice," Jarronn commanded.

Alice's head shot up and her gaze met her king's. "That's two punishments you have now earned." At his frown she quickly lowered her gaze and then knelt in front of Darronn . . . and his incredibly huge erection.

"As your first punishment," Jarronn said, his voice calm but firm, "you will suck Darronn's cock however he pleases, until he comes."

More heat than ever flooded through Alice. *Oh, my god.* Jarronn wanted her to go down on his brother! His frequent comments about fucking her with his brothers came rushing back to her. He'd been preparing her for this all along. And whenever he'd talked about it, the thought of being taken all at once by four gorgeous men had excited her to no end.

"Alice, for your delay you have earned a third punishment." Jarronn's tone was much harsher now. "While in this room you will refer to my brothers as Master Darronn, Master Karn, and Master Ty."

"Slide those lovely lips around my cock, wench," Darronn demanded as he moved his erection closer to her face. "And use your hands, too."

"Yes, Master Darronn." Alice reached for him, not

wanting a fourth punishment added to her list. His cock was a bit thicker than Jarronn's and the head a darker plum color. As she wrapped her fingers around the base, the texture felt a bit different, too, and already a drop of pre-come had beaded at the small hole at the tip. She lowered her head and swirled her tongue over the head.

Darronn sucked in his breath and his cock jerked in her hand. The thought that she affected him and that she was responsible for his erection gave Alice that feeling of empowerment that she'd come to embrace in this world. She slid her mouth over his length and worked one hand along the base in time with her movements. With her free hand she cupped his balls and fondled them.

"I'm going to fuck your mouth, wench." Darronn clenched his hands into Alice's hair. He jerked her head back so that she was looking up at him while he thrust his cock in and out. It hurt as he pulled her hair, yet it felt good, too. Her breasts bounced and the hearts swung at her nipples as he thrust his hips while he watched her with his fierce green eyes that were so like Jarronn's. But everything else about this man was so much different from her king.

Out of the corner of her eye she caught Jarronn's tense features and a glimpse of his huge erection. Her nipples grew tighter to know that he was turned on by watching his brother and her.

Darronn bared his teeth like a tiger and let loose with a growl as he came. His fluid spurted to the back of Alice's throat and she swallowed and sucked on his cock until he pulled his wet member out of her mouth and released his grip on her hair. Like Jarronn, his length was impressive, even when it was spent.

"Very good, Alice." Jarronn's words reminded Alice of her duties as his sub, and she quickly lowered her gaze and resumed the position of respect while still on her knees. "Your second punishment will be to suck Karn's cock, in any manner he chooses."

Alice swallowed. Was Jarronn going to make her give them all head? But strangely enough, the idea actually excited her because she knew it was turning Jarronn on. She could imagine how bad Jarronn was going to want her by the time she finished, and he'd probably fuck her until she couldn't walk.

"Look at me," Karn ordered when he stood in front of her. Alice tilted her head up to look at the black-haired, black-eyed King of Diamonds. "Use only your mouth and tongue, Alice."

"Yes, Master Karn." She kept her hands behind her back and slid his erection into her mouth. Karn used his hands to gently guide her as she sucked and swirled her tongue along his length. "That's it, Alice. You are a beautiful woman and you have a sweet, hot mouth."

She was so aroused and so needy for an orgasm that she wished Jarronn would come up behind her and slide his cock into her while she sucked off Karn.

With a rumbling purr Karn pulled his cock out of Alice's mouth, and his come squirted onto her breasts. He used his hand to milk all his fluid from his cock and onto her chest. Her hands still behind her back, Alice arched into the streams, the feel of his come on her breasts wild and erotic.

"Thank you, Alice," Karn said when he finished. He knelt on one knee and pressed his mouth against hers. When her lips parted in shock, he darted his tongue inside before rising and stepping away.

Jarronn gave a low rumble and Alice wasn't sure if it was anger or approval at Karn's actions. But she wasn't about to look at Jarronn and earn a fourth punishment, so she bowed her head and waited.

To no surprise, Jarronn said, "You will now suck Ty's cock, however he wishes it."

Only when Ty reached her he got down onto the carpeted floor with his feet in Jarronn's direction. Ty folded his hands behind his head and gave her a sexy, devilish grin. "Alice, you're going to position yourself on your hands and knees so that your gorgeous ass is facing me and you're looking right at Jarronn."

"Yes, Master Ty." Alice trembled with excitement while she arranged herself as Ty instructed her to, but she kept her gaze down.

"Slide your mouth over my cock and use your hands," Ty said, "and I want you to watch Jarronn the entire time you're sucking me."

"Yes, Master Ty." Alice's hand shook as she gripped Ty's erection and put her mouth over it at the same moment she looked up at Jarronn.

Oh, dear. He looked ready to kill someone or to fuck her out of her mind. She was hoping it was the latter.

Even though he was obviously turned on by watching his brothers with her, she could tell it was driving him nuts, too.

"Come on," Ty said from behind her. "Faster, Alice."

She kept her gaze on Jarronn as she began sucking Ty in earnest, hoping he wouldn't take too long and that he'd come fast. Her energy was still sky-high from that *eetmi* cake, but her jaws were getting a little sore.

Just as she was getting into a good rhythm and getting used to watching Jarronn's tightly reined lust, something thrust into her anus. Alice's eyes widened and she came to a complete stop.

"Keep going, Alice," Ty said. "I'm just finger-fucking your sexy ass while you suck me."

Jarronn narrowed his gaze, and Alice got moving. Ty slid another finger in and rammed them in and out of her ass while she gave him his blow job. From her peripheral vision she caught the intense expressions of Darronn and Karn, whose cocks had definitely recovered and were rarin' to go again.

The feel of Karn's come drying on her breasts, the swing of the dangling hearts from her nipples, Ty fucking her ass with his finger, Karn and Darronn watching, and Jarronn's intensely aroused stare . . . it all made Alice so incredibly hot that she was afraid she'd climax without Jarronn's permission.

No. She wouldn't come unless he told her she could.

But everything was so intense!

"Yes, gorgeous, that's *it*!" Ty shouted, and thrust his hips toward her face and climaxed. Alice continued sucking him until he ordered her to stop, and then he pulled his fingers out of her ass.

As Ty's cock was sliding out of her mouth, Jarronn abruptly stood. Alice stayed on her hands and knees and looked at his feet, her heart pounding as she wondered what he was going to do to her now.

"You are ready for the bonding, Alice," Jarronn said. "Rise and look at me."

"Yes, Milord." Alice rose to her feet, her ass still tingling from Ty's fingers, and brought her gaze to Jarronn's.

Jarronn tossed Ty a dark look, as if to say, *You did not have permission to enter my woman.* When he turned back to Alice, the possessiveness in Jarronn's icy green gaze was enough to make her pussy spasm.

"I am still disappointed in you, Alice." Jarronn folded his arms across his chest and fought back his raging arousal as he studied his beautiful woman. "You hesitated far too many times. Remember you must obey me without question in anything I request of you."

"I'm sorry, Milord." She lowered her gaze. "It will not happen again."

Using his magic, Jarronn retrieved the red flogger from his quarters, and it appeared in his palm. "Look at me, Alice." He reached out and brushed the soft leather straps along her cheek as her gaze met his again. "Do you understand why you are being punished?"

"Yes, Milord." Her aqua-green eyes glittered with both fear and excitement. He knew she enjoyed the flogger, but this time its use would bring her to that state she would need to be in to perform the mind-bond with all four kings. This bonding would ensure her protection as the future High Queen.

Jarronn guided her to the center of the turret where the large golden ring hung suspended in midair. "Hold on to the ring, Alice."

"Yes, Milord." This time there was no hesitation as she followed his instructions and grabbed hold of the ring. It was positioned just high enough that she had to stretch to grab hold of it.

"Remember all of the rules, Alice." Jarronn set aside the flogger on a nearby couch, then retrieved a red silk scarf with his magic and used the cloth to bind her hands to the ring. "I am confident you won't disappoint me again."

Her expression remained calm, and he knew that her trust in him at this moment was complete. With a flick of his fingers, he produced her blue satin hair ribbon and blindfolded her.

He leaned close and whispered in her ear, "Not a sound, Alice."

Alice relaxed, turning over all control to Jarronn. She couldn't see with the blindfold on, but she could feel and hear everything. A hand brushed her nipples, causing the hearts to dangle wildly, and then Karn murmured, "She is magnificent."

From behind her came Darronn's deep voice as a callused hand caressed her butt cheeks. "A beautiful wench with an ass made to fuck."

Firm lips brushed over hers and she caught the

scent of ale and spice. "A woman made to both fuck and love," Ty murmured, and warm breath caressed her mouth.

"*My* woman," Jarronn growled with both possessiveness and pride in his tone.

Being blindfolded and unable to rely on her sight allowed Alice to hear what was not said along with what was said aloud. These men found her beautiful, and they all wanted her. It was a heady, amazing feeling, and she almost smiled.

The familiar feel of a flogger caressed her breasts. "Alice belongs to me and only me," Jarronn said as the leather straps moved down to her waist. "She will always be mine."

When the first stinging lash landed across her thigh, Alice reflexively jerked against her bonds. She relaxed into every subsequent lash, wanting the pain that melded into rapture. A storm of a climax grew inside her, but she would not come yet. Her orgasm would be her gift to Jarronn when he asked for it.

Each lash landed on a different part of her body. The front of her thighs, the back of them, her ass, her back, her shoulders. Her body was on fire, flames of ecstasy scorching her with every lash. Stronger and stronger they fell, driving her closer and closer to that state of bliss she welcomed like her lover's embrace.

When the lashes stopped, Alice was only partly aware of warm male bodies surrounding her. One pressed close behind, holding her waist, his pole vault of a cock rubbing against her ass. Another male body moved in front of her, his erection poking her belly as she felt him reach up to undo her bonds.

The moment she was released, her body sagged and she would have fallen if it weren't for the man holding her from behind. A tug on her blindfold and then it was gone. In her daze she saw that she was in a Jarronn and Darronn sandwich and she almost giggled, but it was with a smile that she looked into her king's ice-green eyes.

"You are ready now, love," Jarronn murmured, and a thrill skittered through her soul at his endearment. "You were perfection."

He scooped her up, cradling her in his arms, and carried her across the room. His hard chest felt solid, his skin warm, with a light sheen of sweat. Her body was on fire from the lashes and she needed to take Jarronn deep inside her to quench the flames.

When he came to a stop, she saw that he was standing beside the red leather swing she'd noticed earlier. Like the gold ring, the swing was suspended with no visible means of support. To either side of the swing were steps that curved around it in a cozy embrace.

Jarronn nodded to his twin. Darronn gave a smile of satisfaction and threw himself into the swing. From out of nowhere a small jar appeared in his palm, and he used its contents to lubricate his cock before making the jar vanish.

Alice watched him in dazed fascination, and when Jarronn lowered her toward his twin's lap, placing her legs on either side of his, she didn't question him, even in her mind.

"My brother is going to slide his cock into your ass, Alice," Jarronn murmured. "You may speak, but you may not come until I give you permission."

"Yes, Milord," she said even as the tip of Darronn's cock pressed against her anus.

Darronn held on to her hips and brought her down in a swift movement, fully thrusting himself into her ass. She gasped and her eyes widened at the sudden feel of him.

Jarronn moved between her thighs and the possessiveness in his gaze told her he gloried in the sight of her open to and for him alone. The swing was at the perfect height for him to slide right into her. God, she couldn't wait to feel him. But he didn't take her yet. Instead he gestured to Karn, who moved up the stairs along the right side of the swing until his cock was at the same level as her lips.

"Take Karn in your mouth," Jarronn instructed her.

Trembling with excitement, she replied, "Yes, Milord."

Karn slid his hand into Alice's hair and guided his cock into her mouth. In the next moment Ty was on a lower step on the other side of the swing. Her breasts were large enough that he cupped and squeezed them together and could slide his cock between the fleshy globes.

She felt pulled into and pressed against from all

different directions, and she thought she would explode if they didn't start fucking her now.

Jarronn rubbed his cock along her slick folds. "Remember, Alice, do *not* come until I tell you to."

With that he slid into Alice's core, and she cried out around her mouthful of Karn's cock.

All four men began fucking her in a slow, easy rhythm. It was unlike anything she could ever have imagined. It was more than a fulfillment of her fantasy—it was simply unbelievable.

Faster and faster their rhythm increased . . . Jarronn's cock thrusting within her pussy, Darronn filling her ass, Karn plunging in and out of her mouth, and Ty fucking her breasts.

Tears pricked at the back of Alice's eyes, so intense were the sensations and so close was she to orgasm. But she would not climax. She would not disappoint Jarronn.

The men fucked her harder, the smells of their sweat and testosterone and her juices filling the air. She could sense something building within all of them, something more powerful and stronger than just an orgasm.

A rich musk emanated from the men and Alice's eyes widened as her body began to shake and tremble. She sucked Karn's cock harder and moved her hips more frantically between Jarronn and his twin and arched her back so that her breasts pressed even closer to Ty. She had to have them all take her harder and faster, and she had to come before she shattered.

"Now!" Jarronn shouted. "Come for me, Alice!"

The world exploded around her. White-hot fire seared her mind and shot through her body. She was barely aware of Karn's come filling her mouth and her drinking from him even as Jarronn growled and climaxed inside her pussy. Darronn roared and his cock contracted in her ass, and Ty shouted when his fluid spurted over her neck.

Alice's body vibrated with lightning jolts from her climax and from the strange fire that had burned through her mind and body. Instead of lessening, they seemed to grow stronger, until she was certain she could take no more.

In the next moment Jarronn lifted her, his strong arms bearing her away . . . Darronn's cock slid out of her ass, Karn slipped his length out of her mouth, and Ty released his hold on her breasts.

The red velvet room spun and then she was on her back, sinking into the deep carpet and staring up at Jarronn, who had placed himself firmly between her thighs. "From this moment forward you are mine, Alice," he said at the same time he thrust his cock into her. "Only mine."

"Yes, Milord," she whispered, her mind and body hurtling toward oblivion.

On some level she was conscious of his brothers watching as Jarronn fucked her, as he claimed her in front of them. With a cry she climaxed again and again until tears streamed from her eyes. Her king shouted a sound of triumph as he came, but it was faint to her ears as she started to fade.

"I love you, Alice," Jarronn said as she sailed onto another plane. "I love you, my queen."

I love you, Jarronn, she tried to say, but she was slipping away and the words wouldn't reach her lips.

Jarronn's handsome features dimmed, and then everything went dark.

CHAPTER ELEVEN

WHEN ALICE HAD WOKEN AFTER THE BONDing, it had been well into the night. She'd found herself with Jarronn in his bed, his arms wrapped tightly around her. That was well over two Tarok weeks ago, which was something like almost four Earth weeks, and she'd slept with Jarronn every single night since the bonding.

He loved her. He really loved her! And soon, she would be his queen.

Omigod, she was going to be the Queen of Hearts.

After the bonding he had more or less proposed to her—all right, he pretty much *told* her they were joining, in that commanding way of his that caused her to shiver. For two weeks servants had scurried around the castle, making preparations for the ceremony and for Alice's official presentation to Tarok as the High Queen.

Cripes. She was going to be a freaking *queen.*

This evening, though, Alice strolled alone through the rainbow gardens. A smile curved her lips as she lightly ran her fingertips over a deep red bloom that reminded her of a giant daisy. She'd never been so happy in all her life. Jarronn was still her Dom and the rules were still the rules, but she would be serving at his side as queen. Every now and then she would earn a flogging or two, but usually because she deliberately misbehaved.

Alice almost skipped as she walked over the rise to the fountain where she'd first seen Karn, Ty, and Darronn taking Kalina. Her nipples tightened at the memory and she wished that Jarronn were here with her now instead of off worrying about a rogue queen named Mikaela from Malachad. Jarronn had talked a bit to Alice about the evil woman, and she'd overheard him with his brothers on occasion. Right now Jarronn was with his brothers at the kings' jungle meeting place to discuss the problems with the kingdom to the south.

Gradually Alice was learning about the Kingdom of Hearts, Tarok, and this world, and she was finally feeling less overwhelmed about everything. Jarronn and Alice were together most days, but now that he considered her training complete he sometimes left her while he performed his kingly duties. He had a country to rule, and he often teased her that with her at his side all he could think about was sliding deep inside her.

She could live with that.

Usually when Alice wasn't with Jarronn, the sorceress Kalina had been teaching Alice her queenly duties.

But tonight the sorceress had been deep in a trance, and when that happened there was no getting her out of it. So Alice had decided to go for a walk.

She stopped by the fountain and watched water droplets sparkle in the waning sunlight. She closed her eyes and absorbed the feel of air against her naked skin, smells of flowers in the rainbow gardens, sounds of water splashing in the fountain, the rustling of tree leaves, and the soft chirrup of birds.

When she opened her eyes, Alice realized she was facing the very place where she had woken all those weeks ago. A strong urge came over her, drawing her toward the spot. The hearts dangled from her taut nipples and the fine silver chain attached to her collar swayed against her hips as she started toward the location where she had more or less landed in this wonderland.

Jarronn had never really explained how she came to be here, even when she asked. It was one of those things that she was expected to accept, she supposed. The old Alice would have fretted and worried about it, but the new Alice had turned over all control of her concerns to Jarronn. He would protect her and care for her, and in turn she would please him.

Alice came to a stop beneath the tree where she had found herself in wonderland. She tilted her head to look up at the trees. Had she just fallen through some kind of cosmic pudding tunnel to land here? A freak happening?

Her thoughts automatically turned to her sister, and

as always Alice's heart twisted with longing for Alexi. On Earth Alice would have been missing something like six weeks now, and she wondered how Alexi was taking it. Likely, not well. If there ever was a person who had to be in total control, it was Alexi. It would be difficult for her to not have any idea where Alice had gone or how to find her, or even if she *could* be found.

A cold, harsh wind shoved against Alice and she braced her hand against the glossy trunk of the tree. The feathery blue leaves blew wildly above her, and several swirled to the ground in the force of the wind.

Are you ready to go home, Alice? a vaguely familiar feminine voice said in Alice's mind.

She jerked her head up and her skin went cold when she saw a pure white tiger, one with no stripes, maybe twenty feet away. Something in Alice's gut told her this was a weretigress and that she had just spoken in Alice's mind like Jarronn did when he was a tiger.

The tigress was a bit smaller than Jarronn and his brothers, but something about this beast was far more frightening than when Alice had first seen Jarronn as a tiger.

As it—she—approached, Alice braced her hand against the tree and tried to figure out what she should do if the tigress attacked.

I'm here to help you, the feminine voice said. *Don't be frightened, Alice.*

Before she had time to process those statements, the weretigress shape-shifted and it was Alice's nightmare come to life. The Dominatrix from that horrible dream.

She's real.

The woman gave a tolerant smile. Her wheat-blond hair was piled up on her head and she wore the same black catsuit that partially exposed her breasts and the paw print tattoo around her navel. "You may call me Mistress Mikaela. I've come to assist."

Goose bumps prickled along Alice's skin as she realized this must be the Queen of Malachad whom Jarronn and the sorceress had mentioned. But like hell she'd refer to this woman as *Mistress*. "I don't need help from you." Alice raised her chin and clenched her fists at her sides.

With a shake of her head Mikaela held out her hand, and her black whip appeared. Apparently her ability to shape-shift and her powers were identical to those of Jarronn and the other kings.

"No, not identical," the woman said as she toyed with her whip. "I am far more powerful than my brothers. I can even send you back to San Francisco, safe and sound."

Too many things pounded into Alice at once. The woman had read her mind, she'd more or less claimed to be Jarronn's sister, and she'd stated she could send Alice home.

Mikaela took another step forward and Alice forced herself to keep her ground.

"Do you not know how you got here?" Mikaela asked, arching a sculpted brow. When Alice didn't answer, the woman smirked. "Of course Jarronn didn't tell you that he intentionally brought you to Tarok, did he?"

Alice clenched her hands tighter. "Go away. Now."

With a caustic laugh, Mikaela snapped her whip. "Such blind obedience to a man who merely needs you to serve as a breeder for his cubs."

Alice's thoughts whirled, but she refused to doubt the man she loved. She had absolute faith and trust in Jarronn and she knew that no matter what else might occur or what had happened in the past, he loved her as much as she loved him.

"Foolish one. He cares for nothing but the continuation of his people." The woman tilted her head as she studied Alice, as though trying to read more deeply into her mind. "Your sister, on the other hand, is terribly worried about you."

"I've had enough," Alice said in a calm but forceful tone. "I want you to leave."

Mikaela snarled and snapped her whip. The crack met Alice's ears a second before she felt the cruel sting on her thigh. One glance showed blood pouring down Alice's leg, and her gut clenched with fear. This was not like Jarronn's loving swats. No, this woman was brutal and vicious.

"You're an ugly, fat bitch, Alice O'Brien." Mikaela cracked her whip again, and pain seared Alice's other thigh. "Jarronn is using you. Why would he settle for someone like you when he could have anyone he wants?"

This time, Alice could clearly see what Mikaela was attempting to do and there was no way she was going to let this woman have any power over her.

"I don't have time for you." Alice turned her back on the woman and started to walk away.

Mikaela shrieked and the whip cracked in the air behind Alice. Blinding pain tore across her back, wrenching through her, and she stumbled to her knees. She tried to get up, but another lash sent her sprawling facedown on the grassy slope beneath the very same tree she'd landed under all those weeks ago.

The four brothers had spent the evening hours mapping out a battle plan when Jarronn felt the slice of a whip across his thigh. Karn, Darronn, and Ty all cut their gazes to Jarronn, and he knew they'd felt the lash, too.

Alice.

Without a single word, the four kings shifted into tigers and bounded toward the rainbow gardens at a speed that would be dizzying to a mere human.

Jarronn's heart pounded with fear for his woman as he tore through the jungle and felt the second lash. The pain from the first had opened up the mind-bond between Alice and the brothers and he knew it was Mikaela who had dealt the blow. Rage surged through him, hot and blinding. He would break the bitch's neck for harming Alice.

When the third lash fell, a far more vicious slice across the back, Jarronn was determined to tear Mikaela's throat out. They were just below the rise leading to the fountain when the fourth lash sliced open Alice's lower back and Jarronn decided he would claw out the bitch's heart while she was still alive and then shred her throat.

As they crested the rise, he saw Mikaela raise her whip to strike Alice again. Jarronn let loose a roar that likely shook the leaves in every tree in his realm. Mikaela's expression was one of fury as she whirled, shifted into a tiger, and bounded into the woods.

I will kill you for what you have done to Alice! Jarronn shouted at Mikaela in thought-words as he tore after her.

Jarronn closed the distance and had almost reached Mikaela when at least a dozen weretigers attacked him and his brothers from all sides.

In a flurry of fur, claws, and fangs the four kings fought Mikaela's minions while the bitch vanished into the trees. Jarronn took out his fury on the weretigers, slicing the throat of a huge male with his fangs and breaking another one's neck with a powerful swipe of his paw. A third bolted into the trees, and Jarronn turned to help his brothers. In moments the remaining weretigers either had fled or were efficiently eliminated.

Without waiting to see how his brothers had fared in the fight, Jarronn whirled and headed to his mate.

Callused fingers gently stroked Alice's face as she slept, and she snuggled into the touch. Soothing and loving, the soft caress continued, slowly drawing her out of her dreamworld. Warm breath feathered across her lips and she inhaled the rich scent of spice, sandalwood, and man.

"Wake, Alice love," Jarronn murmured in his deep, rumbling voice.

She lifted her eyelids to find she was locked in his embrace, their legs tangled and her breasts pressed tight to his chest. "Good morning, Milord," she murmured, and gave him a sleepy smile.

"Will you forgive me?" His ice-green eyes studied her, a serious expression upon his face. "It is my job to protect you, and I failed. Your injuries . . . I am sorry."

This clearly was one of those times when he wished her to speak with him as an equal. "Hey." Alice ignored the stinging wounds at her back and thighs and reached up and caressed the soft hair of his neatly trimmed beard. "I saw you go after Mikaela. You chased her away and then fought those weretigers. I sort of passed out after that."

He gritted his teeth and his eyes flared with heated fire. "My arrogance allowed me to believe you would be safe in my realm during the day. I never believed she would penetrate my kingdom and physically attack you. Until now her war with us has been through the dreams of my people."

Alice put her fingers to his lips. "Shhh. You came for me, just like I knew you would."

His heart swelled with pride and love for his woman. Clasping her hand in his own, he brought it to his chest. "Your faith and trust in me surely saved your life and the future of our kingdom. Without your trust, the mind-bond would not have worked. She would have spirited you from me and done away with you, and my heart would have died with you."

Her aqua-green eyes were large and luminous. "You have shown nothing but faith, love, and caring to me. How could I not trust you? No matter what that woman said, I know your reasons for your choices must have been important."

Squeezing her hand tight within his own, Jarronn pressed a kiss to her forehead and drank in her sweet smells and the orange blossom scent of her hair and skin. "What did she say to you?" he asked as he pulled away and studied her expression.

"That you purposefully brought me here from my world." Alice's gaze was steady as she looked up at him. "And that your only intention was to have me serve as breeder for your cubs."

A low growl rose up within Jarronn at the words Mikaela had used to attempt to hurt Alice. Yet he saw no anger or concern in Alice's features. Instead her expression remained calm and trusting.

"I did bring you here," he said. "And I would do it a thousand times over again." Jarronn knew it was time to tell her all. He explained the sorceress's prophecy and how Alice had been chosen as his mate.

"The draw of a card?" Alice smiled. "I'm glad. If you hadn't, then I wouldn't be here and I wouldn't be as incredibly happy as I am now."

"How could I have been blessed with such a perfect mate?" he murmured, and brought her hand to his mouth and kissed her knuckles. "If you agree, it would be my greatest joy if you would bear my cubs. It is your free choice, Alice. In this I will not command you. No matter, I will love you."

Alice didn't think it was possible to be so happy, to feel so safe and loved and cherished as she did with Jarronn. "If I was pregnant with your child right now," she said, "I would probably explode with happiness."

Jarronn crushed her to him in a grip so tight that all her air left her in a startled gasp.

Air. Can't breathe.

"Apologies, my love." He released her and smiled. "As I am a weretiger, you will conceive only if I release my seed when we reach simultaneous climax. And that is only if you are in heat."

"Wow." Alice rubbed her hands up and down Jarronn's biceps, over his heart tattoo. "That must make it kind of tough. How would you even know when I'm in heat?"

His long dark hair slid against her skin as he sniffed at the curve of her neck. He placed his hot palm on her hip, drawing her tighter to him so that his erection poked her belly. "When you are in heat it is an aphrodisiac to my senses," he murmured, and laved her throat with his rough tongue. "I can sense it, smell it, feel it."

Alice shivered and moaned as his thigh slid between her legs. "Am I in heat now?"

"No." He made a low purring sound as his mouth moved from her throat to her breasts. "However, I do believe we could use the practice, wench."

She laughed. "Lots and lots of practice, Milord."

He started to move down her body but paused and looked at her with concern. "Your wounds . . ."

With a smile, she replied, "I feel nothing but desire for you."

Alice slid her hands into Jarronn's hair and she whimpered as he teased her breasts, circling her nipples and flicking his tongue against her heart dangles. When he finally laved one nipple she arched her back, begging for more. "My pleasure, wench," he reminded her as he raised his head and gave her a sexy grin. "Do not climax without my permission."

"Yes, Milord." Alice trembled with excitement as Jarronn took control as her Master again. She loved it when he called her wench and when he dragged out her climax, making her so hot that she had the most spectacular orgasms when she was finally allowed to come.

"Grab the bar above your head and spread your thighs for me," he demanded as he licked a trail down her belly. "As wide as you can." He crouched between her thighs as she reached for the bar across the wooden headboard of his bed and spread herself open to him. "Wider, wench. Do not let go of the bar until you have my permission."

She forced her legs wide, feeling deliciously exposed to his gaze. Being forced to hold on to the bar was like being bound, and it made her so hot.

When Jarronn lowered his mouth, he licked her with one broad stroke of his tongue. Alice cried out and arched her back at the exquisite sensations. He slid his hands under her ass and raised her to his mouth.

"May I come, Milord?" she asked when she was so close to the peak she wasn't sure she could hold back.

"No." Jarronn reared up and placed his cock to her core's entrance. He hooked his arms under her knees and raised her up, opening her even wider to him.

"What do you want, wench?" he said, holding himself perfectly still while he waited for her answer.

"Take me, Milord." Her chest rose and fell and her heart pounded. "If it would please you, I wish to be fucked."

"It pleases me, wench." Jarronn growled and drove his cock into her.

She held on to the headboard bar, her breasts bouncing with every thrust of his cock. He clenched his jaw as he plunged in and out of her, his ice-green eyes never moving from her face.

Her body started to flush with heat and she knew her climax was fast approaching. "May I come, Milord? Please!"

He thrust into her again and again, ignoring her request, and she was close, so close, when he finally said, "Come for me, Alice."

Heat and fire burst through her as she came, and Jarronn's growl of release joined hers. His hot come squirted inside her core and Alice thrust her hips against his, wanting more, giving more, until neither could take any more. Jarronn rolled onto the bed taking Alice with him, her hands still clinging to the headboard bar.

Jarronn chuckled as he nuzzled the sweaty skin between her breasts. "You can let go of the bar now."

The room spun as Alice replied in a breathy whisper, "I don't know if I can."

CHAPTER TWELVE

AT LEAST A TRUCKLOAD OF BUTTERFLIES TUM-
bled around Alice's belly as Kalina helped her
prepare for the ceremony. It was Alice's wedding day—or in Tarok it was referred to as her binding
day.

After a hot bath in orchid-scented waters, Alice was
now lying on her back upon a comfortably padded table
in the sorceress's private chambers. Kalina had just finished shaving Alice's mound until it was smooth and
completely hairless again.

"Do not fret, Milady." Kalina's hearts swung from
her nipples as she massaged Alice's mound with special
oil created from a rare jungle orchid. "The ceremony is
beautiful and you will only experience joy on this day."

The tingle in Alice's belly made her bite her lip and
she could only nod in response. Every time the sorceress shaved Alice's mound, it made her so hot and horny
she couldn't wait to get back to Jarronn. But today the

wait would be agonizingly long because everything had to proceed according to this country's traditions.

Damn tradition, anyway.

A smile curved Kalina's full lips and her amber eyes glittered while she massaged more of the fragrant oil onto the rest of Alice's body, starting high on her thighs and lightly brushing her mound. The sorceress seemed to love sensually teasing her, and Alice couldn't say she didn't enjoy it. Often she wondered if Jarronn put Kalina up to it in order to make Alice even hotter for him. Not that she needed any help in that regard.

While she was enjoying the erotic torture of Kalina's massage, Alice's thoughts turned to the day's activities that would start in just a few short hours. During a mysterious binding ceremony that no one would fully explain, Alice would be presented to the people as High Queen of Tarok and as queen over the Kingdom of Hearts. She only wished she knew what the binding ceremony was all about.

The sorceress's small, soft hands and her sensual touch were arousing as she massaged Alice's body, yet relaxing, too. When Kalina finished working the orchid oil onto Alice's legs, belly, breasts, and arms, Alice turned over so that she was facedown on the table. Kalina's hands were truly magic as she methodically massaged Alice from her neck and shoulders, along her back, butt, and legs, and all the way down to her feet and toes.

When the massage was finished, Kalina helped Alice to her feet and told her to sit on a blue-velvet-covered stool in the center of the room. "The king prefers your tresses long and loose," Kalina said as she began brushing out Alice's silky blond hair. "However, for the ceremony I will arrange it in a different fashion."

Alice smiled as she thought about how much Jarronn enjoyed her hair down. Yeah, he loved to wrap his hands in her hair when she sucked his cock or while he was taking her, and she loved how masterfully he handled her.

Kalina's chamber had a kind of mysterious air about it, just like the black-haired sorceress. The walls were cobalt blue and hundreds of candles flickered and danced from the breeze coming through the window. Countless smells filled the room as always, but today the most prevalent were plum spice and hazelnut mixed with the massage oil's orchid scent.

After Kalina finished arranging Alice's hair, she moved behind her and murmured, "You no longer need this," and then Alice felt the red leather collar fall away.

"Why?" Alice put her hand to her bare throat, feeling somehow more naked without the symbol of Jarronn's ownership. "Won't Jarronn be upset?"

The sorceress touched her own collar with her fingertips as she moved in front of Alice. "I, too, will miss mine when it is taken from me." Kalina paused and with quick movements plucked the dangling heart nipple rings from each of Alice's nipples. "And these, too."

Alice gasped but resisted the urge to clap her hands to her breasts. Okay, it sounded ridiculous, but with the collar and nipple rings on she hadn't felt as utterly naked as she did now. But it was more than that . . . she felt somehow disappointed, too.

In her disappointment, she'd missed what Kalina had said, but then it hit her. "What do you mean, when yours are taken?"

With a shrug of one delicate shoulder, the sorceress lowered her eyelids that were covered with the red glitter eye shadow she always wore. "As sorceress I serve the oldest unbound male heir to the High King's throne." She raised her gaze and tossed a strand of her black hair over her shoulder. "Darronn is now the oldest unbound male in Tarok. After the ceremony I will remove King Jarronn's symbols and accept King Darronn's and leave with him for the Kingdom of Spades."

A little of Alice's joy faded. "You mean that you won't be around anymore? You—you're my friend."

Kalina smiled and cupped Alice's cheek. "It pleases me to hear these words from you." She pressed her lips against Alice's and gave her a soft, sweet kiss.

She felt more than a little dazed as the sorceress moved away and retrieved a stack of cloth from on top of one of the room's many crowded tables. Alice forced herself to focus on what Kalina was doing, instead of the kiss.

The cloth she picked up was a turquoise-colored material that glittered like starlight. The sorceress held on to part of it and let the rest fall toward the floor, and Alice saw that it was an exquisite dress. "Your ceremonial gown, Milady," Kalina murmured.

"Oh, my." Alice sighed with delight as she stood and reached out to touch the material. "It's like a Tarok cloud."

"Milord believes it is like your eyes." Kalina smiled. "It is a traditional Tarok ceremonial gown, but he had this one designed especially for you."

With giddy excitement, Alice slipped into the sleeveless ankle-length dress. When she had it on, she was sure the gown had to be on wrong, because the neckline scooped so low that it was *under* her breasts. Not only that, but it also supported them from beneath so that her breasts were high and sticking out as though they were being served a platter. The dress couldn't be on backward because it was backless and dipped all the way to the top of the crack in her ass.

Alice glanced up from her platter of boobs to look at the sorceress. "Where's the rest of the dress?"

Kalina retrieved a small pot from a nearby table and dipped her finger into the substance. "It fits perfectly," she said as she dabbed the creamy rouge onto one of Alice's nipples, causing it to harden at once. "Of course you shan't be wearing it for long."

Heat infused Alice's cheeks as it hit her that she was meant to show off her, ah, assets and that Kalina was making them more obvious.

Once Kalina finished fussing with Alice's dress and hair, the sorceress drew her into a dark corner of the room, in front of a large, ornate mirror. "You shall make such a lovely queen, Milady."

Alice hardly recognized herself.

She looked like a princess—a queen, even. Her white-blond hair was piled high on her head, with a few ringlets arranged beside her face and tumbling to her shoulders. A turquoise ribbon was woven through the curls piled atop her head.

Her almond-shaped eyes were still her best feature, and the dress she wore made them look even larger and more luminous. Of course she was still full figured, but now she realized her voluptuous shape was perfect . . . her full breasts and sumptuous curves were made for Jarronn to hold tight in his arms. The glittery, almost sheer fabric of the dress's skirt showed a hint of her ample thighs.

When she turned from the mirror to look at Kalina, the sorceress looked as proud as Alexi would have if she'd been here.

Although the boob-lift and nipple exposure would have needed some explanation, not to mention the rouge.

On impulse, Alice hugged the naked sorceress. "Thank you," she whispered as she brushed her mouth across Kalina's soft lips. "For everything."

Jarronn adjusted his red ceremonial kilt, hoping his cock would behave and not tent the fine material through the duration of the ceremony. The fire in his loins would surely set the cloth aflame if his woman did not present herself soon.

He stood on the dais at the head of the castle's

private ceremonial chamber, beside the throne and ceremonial devices. He folded his arms across his chest as he surveyed the small crowd of twenty-six weretigers and weretigresses who had gathered to witness Jarronn taking his mate. Those in attendance were in various states of dress and undress, although everyone wore some kind of finery, whether it was a jeweled collar or silken kilt. Clothing was of little importance to the people of Tarok and, more often than not, worn in a manner that would be arousing to their partners.

Outside the castle, Jarronn's warriors were on alert for any intrusion by Mikaela or her minions. He would not put it past the bitch to interrupt the day he would bind his queen to him. But he would not allow thoughts of his sister to ruin such a fine day. He and his brothers had put the strongest warding on the castle and all would be prepared if she struck again.

Soft light glowed from orbs placed around the room as well as from red and white candles. Bloodred carpeting covered the chamber's floor, matching the red velvet divans and settees. Red velvet drapes shrouded the windows, ensuring that the events within would remain private, as was weretiger tradition.

In the back of the room, Ty had cornered a lovely brunette weretigress whom the youngest king would no doubt be fucking soon enough. Darronn reclined on a settee with two wenches in his lap, and he alternately fondled and sucked on their breasts.

Karn stood in the wide doorway, his stance wide, his arms folded across his chest. As always, an unreadable expression masked his features as his gaze touched upon every person in the room.

Outside the doors, Kalina approached Karn, who straightened, then followed her out of the room. Jarronn's gut clenched while he waited for his brother's return.

It was time.

If Alice had thought she was nervous before, it was nothing compared to how she felt when Karn took her hand to lead her to the ceremonial chambers. He was bare chested as always but clothed in black pants and boots, his hair falling across his shoulders and shimmering like the blue-black of a raven's wing.

Kalina took Alice's other hand and gave her a reassuring smile. The sorceress wore only her red leather collar and nipple rings, which made Alice miss her own even more. Funny how she'd become so accustomed to being naked that it felt strange wearing any kind of clothing.

Karn and Kalina interlocked their fingers with Alice's and raised their linked hands so that both of Alice's were above her head. Her heart pounded faster and the butterflies in her belly decided to go ballistic.

They rounded the corner from the hallway, and a hush fell over the ceremonial room the moment the trio stepped over the threshold. Alice's vision blurred and the crowd faded from the edges of her sight so that the only person in the room she was truly aware of was Jarronn.

He stood upon a red carpeted dais before a massive

mahogany and red velvet throne. Jarronn's eyes focused entirely on her, his powerful shoulders thrown back and his bearded chin raised. He clenched his fists at his sides and his muscles gleamed like a bodybuilder's, as if coated in oil. He wore a kilt that revealed his athletic thighs . . . and from the way it was tented, he was very pleased to see her.

Karn and Kalina started forward, startling Alice from her Jarronn-induced trance. As her bare feet sank into the thick carpeting, she was vaguely aware of murmurs and soft sounds of approval, but mostly her focus was on her king.

When they stopped before the bottom step of the dais, Karn and Kalina bowed and slipped away, leaving Alice alone before Jarronn. She shivered at the predatory look in his eyes, but she kept her gaze level with his. Without the symbols of his ownership around her throat and at her nipples, she felt lost yet certain that at this moment she was not supposed to act her role as his sub. Not yet, anyway.

Jarronn stepped down from the dais and stood within a hairsbreadth from Alice. Her nipples tightened and the heat of his body radiated toward her. His masculine scent of sandalwood and spice filled her senses—she only hoped that he didn't release any of his *tigri* pheromones, because crowd or not, she'd jump him in a New York minute.

"Undress for your king," Jarronn commanded in his powerful voice, and Alice caught her breath.

Shivers scattered throughout her body and her nipples

tightened. Even though she was aware that a roomful of people were watching, Alice didn't hesitate to obey her king. She pushed down first one shoulder strap and then the next. The shimmering gown slid down her and landed in a pool around her feet.

A devastatingly sensual purr emanated from Jarronn. He raised his fist and opened it, and a long strand of alternating rubies and diamonds lay upon his palm, sparkling in the room's soft lighting. It appeared to be a necklace, although there were small rings at each end, and attached to the rings were hearts made from rubies.

"As my queen, you will wear this symbol of my ownership," Jarronn stated. "Do you accept my chain, Alice?"

"Yes, Milord." Alice's voice rang out clear with her conviction.

Jarronn pinched one of her rouged nipples and it hardened even more. Taking the strand of rubies and diamonds, he slid the ring at one end over her nipple and then repeated the process with her other nipple. The glittering strand draped from one breast to the other, and the hearts made of rubies dangled and bounced lightly against her breasts like soft kisses.

The nipple chain was beautiful, and Alice loved how it looked—an erotic kind of necklace for her breasts.

When Alice raised her head to look at Jarronn again, he kept his face expressionless as he held out his hand. She caught her breath at the gorgeous band of diamonds that appeared in his palm. It was at least an inch wide and as long as her leather collar had been.

Along the band were large hearts made from dozens of faceted rubies, and a very fine linked chain attached to it that spilled over his palm. The ring at the end swung back and forth like a pendulum, in time with the pounding of Alice's heart.

"As my queen, my collar will grace your neck." His voice lowered: "Do you accept my collar, Alice?"

She took a deep breath. "Yes, Milord."

Jarronn moved behind her and she trembled from both nervousness and excitement as his kilt-covered erection brushed against her backside. He moved the loose ringlets of her hair aside, slipped the collar around her neck.

"You are my possession, Alice," Jarronn's voice rang out as he fastened the collar. The silver chain slid down her back and settled within the crack of her buttocks. "You are mine to cherish and protect, and to love."

Wow. Alice tingled with excitement from head to toe. *Talk about one hell of a wedding ring.*

"Face me," Jarronn commanded, his cock aching so badly he wanted to forgo tradition and just take her now. But that would come . . . just not soon enough to suit him.

When she turned around, Jarronn folded his arms across his chest. "Kneel."

Gracefully Alice lowered herself to the floor, and he was pleased to see that she assumed the position of respect automatically. He was aware of the excitement rippling through the weretigers in attendance and could smell their collective arousal.

"To show your submission to your king," Jarronn said, "you will use your hands and your mouth on my cock until I spill my seed into your throat."

He sensed her surprise, but she did not disappoint him and did not hesitate. Alice raised her head and pushed aside the opening to his kilt. Grasping his cock with one hand, she caressed his bollocks with her other. Her mouth slid over his erection, and by the skies he thought he would come at once if he didn't maintain his control.

Jarronn clenched his hands in her tresses and tugged at the turquoise ribbon. Her hair tumbled over her naked shoulders. He tilted her head back so that her eyes focused on him as he watched his cock move in and out of her hot mouth. His collar glittered at her neck, and her nipple chain sparkled from breast to breast. The signs of his ownership of this woman, and her complete acceptance and trust in him, threw him into a fierce climax. Candle flame flickered around the chamber as he roared his release into his mate's mouth, as though a wind had suddenly burst through the room.

Once Alice had taken his seed, he instructed her to stand. She eased to her feet and assumed the position of respect.

A part of Alice was amazed that she had just given Jarronn a blow job in front of a roomful of people. But what really was incredible was how much it turned her on.

"You have pleased me greatly this day, Alice." Jarronn reached up and caressed her face, and she leaned into his touch, needing it. "We will now perform the last act of the binding ceremony, and you will then be my queen."

One more step. Okay, she could do this.

He stepped aside, and even with her lowered gaze she saw a golden bar hovering in midair beside him, one that she was certain hadn't been there before. "Brace your hands on the bar," he ordered her.

The fine silver chain of her new collar slid over Alice's shoulder as she leaned over and grasped the cool metal. Jarronn instructed her to stretch farther from the bar and to widen her stance as far as she could. Her breasts hung down and the ruby and diamond nipple chain swung between them.

Alice was highly aware of the fact that an entire roomful of people had a view of her ass and her shaved pussy, but again it excited her. One thing she'd never thought was that she could be a closet exhibitionist, but she'd just re-formed that opinion.

Jarronn moved out of her line of sight. Her skin tingled in anticipation of the flogger against her ass and she was so turned on that she was afraid she would come at once, and she didn't want to disappoint him. Instead, she felt his erection push against her folds, and he said, "You are my possession, Alice. And you are my queen."

With those words he thrust into her. A cry of sheer ecstasy escaped her. *Omigod,* Jarronn was taking her in front of a roomful of people.

And she loved it.

Her king gripped her hips and plunged in and out

of her hot core. Sensation after sensation rippled through her. Everything swirled and blurred . . . sights, sounds, smells, and the feel of her king as he took her as his queen.

Just as she was about to beg him to let her come, Jarronn murmured, "You may come, Alice."

Her cry was a choked sob, a sound of pleasure experienced that was so sweet it bordered on pain. Spasm after spasm rocked her body and if she hadn't been clinging so tightly to the bar she would have crumpled into a boneless heap on the rich carpeting. Jarronn's roar was followed by the hot rush of come in her core.

As she struggled to find her breath, Jarronn wrapped his arms around her waist, leaned close to her ear, and whispered, "I love you, Alice."

Jarronn slid his cock from his mate, scooped her in his arms, and stood at the head of the ceremonial chamber. Alice wrapped her arms around his neck and clung to him, snuggling against his chest.

"I present you with the High Queen of Tarok and queen over the Kingdom of Hearts!" he shouted. "If you all trust me as much as my queen, our kingdom will thrive once more."

Everyone in attendance applauded and gave enthusiastic shouts. Even as Jarronn carried his queen from the room, most of the weretigers were already fucking. The orgy would last well into the night, but Jarronn had no intention of sharing his woman beyond tradition. Now that the ceremony had been completed and Alice had passed every test required of her, she was his to keep as his own. He wasn't about to share her again.

When he reached the king's chambers, Jarronn placed Alice on his bed and immediately positioned himself between her thighs. She clasped her hands behind his neck and smiled up at him, and she was so beautiful he could barely speak.

She slid her fingers in his hair and caressed his nape. "I'm so happy you found me, Jarronn."

He gave her a soft kiss and pulled back. "If I could grant you any wish, what would it be?"

Alice bit the inside of her cheek as she was wont to do when she was considering something. "I have two wishes, really. Although I don't know that either can be granted."

Jarronn brushed his lips over her cheek. "Tell me, my love."

Alice looked a little sad as she replied, "If it is somehow possible to let my sister know I'm okay, or to bring her here, my happiness would be almost complete."

"This may be difficult, as you expected, but I promise to see what I can do." He retrieved an item from the vault and then brought his hand between them so that she could see what lay on his palm.

"My bracelet!" She grinned. "May I keep it? Alexi gave it to me for our eighteenth birthday."

"I was merely keeping it for you until after your training and the ceremony." Jarronn pulled one of her arms from around his neck, then slid the bracelet onto her wrist. He kissed the tip of her nose, delighted in the happiness in her eyes. "What else would please you?"

"Well . . ." Alice moved her arm back around his neck and he felt her bracelet rub against his skin. She bit her lip as she hesitated, but when Jarronn raised one eyebrow she plunged ahead. "You're a weretiger, and our children will be, too, so you will all live far beyond my lifetime."

She dropped her gaze, and when he hooked a finger under her chin and forced her to look up at him he saw that her eyes glittered with tears. "I wish," she said very slowly, as though it was difficult for her to speak, "I wish I could live long enough to see our children grow up and have children of their own. And I—I wish I could be with you throughout your days."

"Sweet Alice." Jarronn smiled, his heart and soul so full of love for his queen. "The first time I took you as my mate and released the *tigri* pheromones the process was started."

She stilled. "Process?"

With a slow nod, Jarronn said, "Eventually you shall become a weretigress."

"No kidding?" Alice's body tensed and her face lit up with hope. "That means I'll live longer and all that other stuff? And I'll be able to shape-shift, too?"

Jarronn couldn't help but grin. "Yes, my love."

The weretigress already brewing within her stirred, and she pulled him down for a long and hard kiss.

When he pulled away from the kiss, Jarronn's eyes locked with Alice's and he slid his cock into her quim.

Even as she gasped with pleasure, he growled and stated, "You are mine, Alice O'Brien. You belong to me."

Slowly he made love to her, driving them both beyond their limits. Further and further he pushed them both until they climaxed together in an explosion of passion and love.

As they floated down together, Alice sighed and murmured, "I love you, Jarronn."

Jarronn kissed her sweet lips and replied, "And I love you, my Queen of Hearts."

EPILOGUE

I<small>T WAS MIDNIGHT BY THE TIME THE TAXI PULLED</small> up to Alexi's pastel blue San Francisco town house. She and Annie had enjoyed a relaxing evening of several courses, from shrimp cocktail, to clam chowder, to Caesar salad, then grilled salmon, cheesecake for dessert, and coffee with Baileys afterwards. Alexi had enjoyed a couple of glasses of beer and wine during dinner and had managed to keep up her good buzz.

For a fraction of a second when she looked up at the dark town house a sense of loneliness bled through Alexi and she wished she wouldn't be alone for at least one night. But she shoved it away, gave Annie a quick hug good-bye, and climbed out of the cab.

"Get some rest, y'hear?" Annie said as Alexi stood outside the car's door. "Need me to walk you to the door?"

"Okay and nope, I'm fine." Alexi gave her cousin a smile and tried not to wobble on her heels so Annie wouldn't realize just how tipsy she still was. "You made this night *so* much easier to get through."

Annie pushed her glasses up her nose and returned Alexi's smile. "For both of us."

After she shut the car's door, Alexi watched the taxi pull away until its red taillights disappeared over the hill.

With a sigh she turned, her purse slapping against her hip beneath her jacket. She tottered up the steps to the town house she'd been renting since Alice disappeared. It was supposed to have been a surprise for Alice—one of Alexi's law partners had taken a position in New York City and agreed to rent the two-story town house to them at a rock-bottom rate. The day that Alice vanished, Alexi had finalized the deal. The first week after Alice's disappearance, while she searched for her twin, Alexi had hired movers to bring all of Alice's belongings from that little apartment she'd lived in with her asshole of an ex-fiancé. Everything had been moved in and was ready for when Alexi found her sister.

But she never did.

Alexi grasped the old-fashioned brass door handle when she reached the small concrete landing and breathed deeply of the smells of ocean and fresh-cut grass. The sound of a foghorn floated through the night along with the clang of a ferry's bell.

After unlocking the door, she let herself into the dim interior and stood in the foyer while she locked the door behind her. As she slipped her jacket from her shoulders, familiar odors of cinnamon potpourri and lemon furniture polish surrounded her.

But then Alexi caught scents that didn't belong, and she dropped her jacket to the carpeted floor in a rush, freeing her arms. Unfamiliar smells that set her senses on alert because they didn't belong in her home . . . wildflowers, sunshine, and a fresh mountain breeze.

Her purse still hung from her shoulder, and she slipped her hand inside until her fingers met the cool Mace canister. Hair prickled at her nape while she withdrew the canister and then slowly let her purse slide to the carpeted floor, where it landed with a soft thud. Her heart pounded, and the pleasant buzz she'd had vanished.

An eerie blue glow flared from the direction of Alexi's bedroom.

Anger burned in her gut. Someone was in her home and she was going to kick the person's ass. She might not know martial arts like her aunt Awai, but Alexi worked out, she had Mace, and she had a hell of a temper that more than made up for it.

Mace held high in her left hand, Alexi gritted her teeth and silently eased down the plush carpeted steps and through the living room. She clenched her right hand into a fist, prepared to deck the sonofabitch once she nailed him with the Mace.

All her senses were on high alert, and her ankles didn't even wobble in the killer heels. When she reached the bedroom door she waited a second, then peeked around the door frame.

A giant mirror stood where her bed should be. An incredibly beautiful mirror with an ornate frame that glittered in the strange blue glow of her bedroom. Sparkles flashed amongst the blue misty glow, looking as though Tinkerbell had come for a visit.

What the hell?

Anger and confusion mingled with curiosity as Alexi moved toward the mirror. The bead fringe along her blouse caressed her belly as a breeze seemed to come from *inside* the mirror and out into the bedroom. Her steps faltered and she wondered if maybe she'd gotten a whole lot more buzzed than she'd originally thought. She had to be hallucinating . . . all of this.

When she finally reached the mirror she stood face-to-face with her reflection. Her almond-shaped turquoise eyes, her auburn hair, her hand held high, still gripping the Mace. What was she going to do, Mace her mirror image?

The whole moment was bizarre and surreal, and Alexi was sure she'd lost her grip on reality. Hell, maybe her sanity, too. She let the canister slip from her fingers and it gave a soft thunk as it landed on the carpet. The gold bracelet at her wrist glittered in the room's eerie light as she raised her hand and placed her palm flat against the mirror's surface. It was smooth but surprisingly warm to her touch.

It sure didn't feel like a hallucination.

Her reflection rippled and changed and Alexi's knees almost gave out.

A mountain meadow appeared, surrounded with thick forest to the left, a ridge of mountains to the right, and lots of wildflowers scattered through thick grass. A cool breeze washed over Alexi, fluttering the bead fringe at her belly and chilling the gold tiger charm at her navel. In the distance water tumbled down a steep mountainside and she heard the rumble of the falls and heard birds twittering. Rich scents swept over her with the breeze . . . smells of pine, damp forest loam, wildflowers, and fresh water.

Okay, she was certifiable. Call the funny farm, because Alexi O'Brien had done lost it. No more beer for her—crappy-tasting stuff anyway. She might as well just curl up on the floor, take a nap, and sleep it off.

A man moved into her mirror view, and Alexi thought she was going to scream.

That or orgasm, because he was the most gorgeous, as well as the most dangerous-looking, man she'd ever seen . . . and his penetrating green eyes were staring right at her, as if he could *see* her.

Alexi's nipples tightened beneath her scanty midriff top. *Damn* this was one fine hallucination.

The man held up a golden playing card and the muscles of his bare chest and arms rippled with power. His features were strong and chiseled and his long dark hair stirred around his shoulders in the breeze. He looked bad to the bone, from the gold earring he sported in his left ear, to the tattoo of a spade on his left wrist, to—*hold on*—that one hell of a package between his powerful black-clad thighs.

She sucked in her breath and pressed her palm tighter to the mirror. *Damn. If he were real I'd fuck him in a heartbeat.*

The hallucination man's lips quirked and Alexi thought she'd climax just from the sinfully sensual movement.

Time to get out the vibrator.

With a twist of his fingers, the golden card vanished. On his side of the mirror, he raised his hand and placed his palm against Alexi's.

Shock tore through her at the feel of his warm, callused hand against her palm. But when his fingers interlocked with hers Alexi gasped and tried to pull away, but he was too powerful.

The man tugged, and she stared in horrified fascination as her hand and wrist slipped *into* the mirror.

She struggled for real then, fighting to get away from his grip. "Let me go, you sonofabitch!"

A predatory rumble rose up from the man and he yanked her arm. Alexi screamed as she pitched forward and through the mirror.

First, Alexi was taken.
Now, she will be claimed...

King Darronn prefers his women submissive.
Alexi, his future queen, is anything but.
Whatever it takes, Darronn intends to convince
the fiery and spirited Alexi that her
body, heart, and soul belong to him.

 St. Martin's Griffin

She Loves Hot Reads.com

Your online one-stop for all things hot in women's fiction—whether you like historical, paranormal, contemporary, or suspense, we're here to give you a taste of everything!

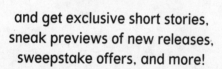

JUST CLICK

and get exclusive short stories,
sneak previews of new releases,
sweepstake offers, and more!

Weekly updates so you don't get bored...
because we know *you love hot reads*.

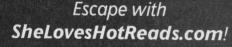